Song

A TRUE LOVE NOVELLA

of Joy

FaytheWorks Publishing | *Faith works together in Christ.*^{TM}

Song of Joy

© 2025 by Renée Allen McCoy

E-book ISBN: 978-1-960169-15-0
Paperback ISBN: 978-1-960169-16-7

The True Love Series

Unquenchable

Many waters cannot quench love,
nor can the floods drown it...
Song of Solomon 8:7

Chapter One

"I CAN'T BELIEVE YOU did this." Joy's voice quivered through clenched teeth. "How could you do this to me?" She squinted as if trying to figure out who the man was standing in front of her. With trembling hands, her quiet composure quickly spiraled into fiery rage. "I've defended you to everybody!" She exploded on him, striking his chest with a powerful shove backwards. "After almost a whole year, this is how you repay me for all that I've done for you?"

Rico stumbled, but quickly regained his footing. "I never meant to get you involved. You've got to believe me." He anxiously fidgeted with the keys in his right pocket.

"*Believe you*? Did you just say *believe you*?" She cautiously took a step toward him, her skin soaked with sweat. "I've believed you for months and look at where it's gotten me." Joy needled her finger into the crevice of his shoulder, irritating a recent injury.

Rico stepped back and put his hand over his shoulder, wincing in pain.

"I practically put everything on the line for you and this is what I get in return?" Her eyes welled with tears. "How dare you bring that stuff in my house!" Joy shouted. "I found traces of white powder in the bathroom and small baggies in the side drawer. Do you want me to get kicked out of school? Do you want the police busting down my door?"

Rico looked away from her as he snatched his black notebook from a nearby desk. He flipped through the pages before extending the book with symbol-marked pages in Joy's direction.

"See for yourself," he urged her. "When I tell you that your name is nowhere, I'm telling you the truth." Rico revealed to her his use of burner phones and public WiFi spots for anonymity. "I don't write anybody's name down. When you loaned me that money, anybody can see that it was legit."

Joy snatched the notebook away from him and squinted as she feverishly flipped through the pages. "Are you crazy? I didn't sign up to date a drug dealer!" She sucked her teeth and slammed the notebook onto a nearby coffee table. "You borrowed money and have yet to pay me back! I trusted you..." Her anger inadvertently revealed her weakness.

"You *can* trust me, Joy." He dared to brace his hands on her shoulders, trying to calm and reassure her. "I'm sorry that I got you mixed up in this, but I just needed the money to float me for a while. When I got pulled over for speeding and the cops saw all that cash on me, they confiscated it. You know I couldn't show up for the court case. How could I explain having all that money on me? I counted that as a loss." He sighed. "Look, I can make the money back, I just need a little time."

Joy's eyes shifted from his to the packed suitcase partially obscured behind a coat rack near the front door. "A little time, huh? For what, Rico?" She knocked his arms away as her chest heaved with anger. "To run back to Cali?"

Rico's shoulders lowered as he avoided eye contact with her. Joy watched as he retreated to another part of the room and swept random notes from the corner desk into a waiting leather satchel. Only seconds ticked past before he stood at the threshold of the front door, gripping the handle of a suitcase at his side. His favorite brown school bag, the one now bulging from its contents, rested across his tall wiry body.

"My flight leaves in an hour and a half," he said to her. "Call you later?"

Her eyes held questions that defied a response.

"*Okay*?" He insisted on an answer, walking closer to her.

Infuriated by his actions, Joy folded her arms and refused to respond. Rico leaned in and tried to kiss her on the cheek. She snapped her head in the opposite direction and scoffed.

With a slight nod he acknowledged her anger and edged away. As he turned, Rico inadvertently bumped into the weathered console table. When the narrow legs of the shelf shifted, he flinched as the ornamental glass filled with seashells and sand crashed to the floor. Joy stared as the sand poured onto the hardwood.

"I'm sorry, Joy." He met her bitter glare. "I didn't mean to do that."

Joy ignored his apologies as she reached for the broken pieces of glass that bore a message and the engraved letters of their names: *Rico and Joy, Always & Forever.*

Before she could fully form the sentences in her mind to respond, he added, "I have to go. I can't miss my flight." Rico hurriedly grabbed the notebook she had discarded only moments before with one hand and the handle to his suitcase with the other.

"Don't come back." Joy smeared tears from her cheeks as she watched him open the front door. "I don't ever want to see you again." She swallowed hard and gritted her teeth. "I mean it. Either you fix this now or walk out that door forever."

"Joy, I am going to fix this," he pleaded. "I'm going to get everything back to you. You know me. I'm good for it."

Joy held up a hand to silence him. "I'm tired of the games, Rico. Fix this now or I'm done." It was her last attempt to recoup what she had foolishly given to him. To keep her parents out of her business, Joy was hesitant to dip into her joint account with them that was slated as an emergency fund to cover her losses.

Rico sighed and watched as headlights from his rideshare pulled into the driveway of Joy's townhome. After an awkward balancing act while shuffling out the door, he briefly met her gaze and without hesitation disappeared into the night.

Chapter Two

IT TOOK ALMOST HALF the night for Joy's seething anger to subside. She was hurt, confused, but angry more than anything. Aside from the money her parents had given her access to, Joy's separate bank account was nearly drained because of her generosity towards a thief. She was now able to admit that she had played the fool for him. Many signs had presented warnings of what a bad relationship it was, but Joy was hopeful that her suspicions would be unfounded. Unfortunately, she was wrong.

When she met Rico in a class roughly a year and a half ago, he was one of the region's top cross-country runners on the collegiate circuit. They easily gravitated to one another. Joy had proudly cheered him on at several of his track meets, and Rico often shared with her his aspiration to compete on a professional level. His commitment to the sport was admirable, so Joy surmised he was well on his way to fulfilling that dream. It wasn't until he was abruptly cut from the team this past season that she saw a downward spiral.

After they became an item, Joy realized that their relationship lacked a deep spiritual connection. When they met, she believed him when he said that he had accepted Jesus Christ as Lord and Savior. As time passed, though, his actions spoke volumes over his words. She soon noticed that his lifestyle didn't line up with his confession of faith. She recognized that Rico's acceptance of God being his Savior was not met with the same enthusiasm when it came to God being his Lord. Having been raised in a Christian home, Joy understood the necessity of both.

Just a few short months after his graduation, Joy now recalled something his mother had said following the ceremony: *It's time to stand on your own two feet.* The conversation quickly changed, but now in hindsight Joy realized this must've meant that she was cutting him off financially. Weeks later was the first time he ever asked her for money. Joy believed his promise of repayment, but now those thoughts played in her mind like a broken record of lies.

"So, you mean to tell me that he left you holding the bag?" Tiana, Joy's friend from high school, questioned. "Just like that, he's gone."

"Girl, yes. And I'm not even sad he's gone. I actually feel like I'm better off. I can't believe I wasted almost a year of my life with him." Joy plopped onto the tufted gray blend loveseat positioned between two ceramic wall sconces. It perfectly framed a large bay window of the townhome they shared in the heart of Simpson, a booming college town located in Alabama, just a few blocks away from campus. "And to think I was *so* close to introducing him to my family."

"I'm glad you didn't do that." Tiana grunted as she pulled a basket full of clothes towards her. "I don't think you've ever taken anyone home to Lewiston. *Ever.*"

"Can you blame me? After seeing how things went down between Charity and the issues Elisha went through with that stalker, it took a miracle for Ma to let me out of her sight. Do you think I was going to tell her anything about my love life?"

Tiana smirked. "So, was it really love?"

Joy chuckled in response, relieved that Tiana hadn't witnessed the breakup. It was bad enough that she had defended Rico multiple times to friends, whether it was his lack of support when she was presented with departmental honors for academics her junior year or simply not showing up to exclusive banquets where he was her plus one. Truthfully, their relationship was over long before the fallout last night. Although it was a rough night for Joy, she was grateful for the call she received this morning that accelerated her healing process.

"What's that laugh supposed to mean?" Tiana folded a pair of athletic pants as she raised her eyebrows. "What are you giggling about?"

It was one of those days for her. Joy had to laugh to keep from crying. She had done enough of that the night before. "Well, I *was* into him, but I wouldn't say that it was love." Joy's demeanor dimmed into a pensive gaze as she tapped her finger on the armrest of the loveseat. "I mean, I liked him a lot, but there was just something about him that kept me from going to the next level, if you know what I mean. And now I know why."

"To the next level?" Tiana gave her a knowing eye. "No, I don't know what you mean. What exactly are you saying? Do tell." She flipped her shoulder length hair to her back and widened her eyes.

Joy waved her hands, instantly redirecting her friend's thoughts. "No, nothing like that, thank God. He was such a scam artist." She was too embarrassed to disclose that she had found out that he was a broke junkie too, which explained why he was kicked off the track team. "Besides, I've had two sisters go through their own dating drama and I've learned from their mistakes and still learning from my own. Anyway, I'm waiting until I'm married before taking *that* step with any man. The spiritual aspect is reason enough, but I'm not trying to get pregnant."

Tiana nodded. "I hear you. You're still thinking about Michelle, huh?"

"Yeah... we were supposed to be here at college together. Something we had planned since middle school. When she got pregnant after our first Christmas break freshman year, I knew she was going to have to go back home. Her mother was not about to take care of the baby for her. Ms. Sabrina was more than willing to help, but she wasn't going to takeover."

"Hm, I'll give it to her, she stayed and finished out that semester before summer break." Tiana referenced Michelle's morning sickness and constant runs to the doctor for prenatal checkups in between studying for classes. "But there was no way she could've taken care of him here at school without extra help."

"Nope. But I'm glad that my little Godson, Clayton, is okay. His father is such a deadbeat." Joy sucked her teeth and grimaced. Not only was she not trying to get pregnant like her best friend, but she wasn't trying to get an STD either. Joy was more upset that he had left her bestie with chlamydia. Michelle told her that in confidence, so that part she kept to herself. "I feel bad for her because she really did love him."

"Yeah, I'm sure she did. I remember how much she used to talk about him. They were *always* together our senior year in high school." Tiana mused about the days they walked through the halls of Lewiston Springs High School in Mississippi. "I'm glad she transferred enrollment to the local college and didn't give up on getting her degree."

"No, I made her promise me that she'd never give up." Joy glanced at the picture of Michelle and now two-year old Clayton on a nearby shelf. He was a spitting image of his irresponsible father. If Michelle wasn't telling her about the missed visits they had scheduled, she was griping about how much Justin didn't provide for their child.

"Is she still going to be able to visit before classes start at the end of the month?"

"I'm not sure. Clayton was on antibiotics for an ear infection, so I don't know."

"Oh, the joy of motherhood," Tiana groaned. "Now I see what my mother was talking about. There is no way I could have the life I have now with a baby in tow."

"But her life isn't over. Michelle is doing great despite all that she's gone through," Joy said, defending her best friend. "They're going to be okay."

"Oh, yeah. I wasn't trying to say that she couldn't do it, I was just saying that—"

"I know what you were saying, Tee." Joy grunted under her breath. "I get it."

The two women shared uncomfortable glances.

The three-bedroom townhouse where they now lived was supposed to be a spot for all three of them throughout their college years. Although it was an investment for Joy since her family bought the place, she rented it out to friends instead of strangers. Her parents, Gerald and Margaret, were set against her living off-campus fresh out of high school, but when a tornado wiped out a large dormitory a couple months before their arrival they had to find lodging off-campus. With friends they approved of, and a gated community with twenty-four-hour security, Gerald and Margaret agreed to allow it after witnessing the growth and maturity in Joy since her car accident in high school.

When Michelle moved out, Joy converted that bedroom into an office with a convenient Murphy bed for visitors. Thanks to her brother, Joshua, and his real estate acumen, Joy was thrilled about the equity she had accrued in the home since moving in three years ago.

"We're officially seniors in college." Tiana drew a smile from Joy. "Can you believe that we'll be graduating come spring?"

"Hardly." Joy smiled in reflection. "Zachary is not going to be happy about me changing my career goals, especially after setting up that internship for me a while back."

"Not to mention the amount of time he spent with you this summer."

"Okay, you don't have to rub it in." Joy smirked. "Don't get me wrong, the experience was great. I still enjoy watching sports and listening to the after-game interviews and commentaries, but..."

"It's just that you enjoy being behind the camera," Tiana said, finishing her sentence.

"Yeah, I have for a while now," Joy confessed. "I don't know...I guess after hearing about how my mother went off on Charity when she changed her major, I felt obligated to follow through with what I had already started. She'll be happy that I didn't change my major, only my minor."

"So, is this *her* degree or yours?"

Joy didn't answer, she just gave a knowing glance. It was no secret what was expected of her growing up. She was trained in etiquette classes and often attended formal events with her parents. It was something she had grown accustomed to after her older siblings left home. Joy often felt like an only child after her brothers and sisters had gone on to start their individual lives. Her upbringing was quite different from theirs, lonely at times, but nonetheless, fostered in love.

The camera lens often fascinated her. Although it started as a hobby during freshman year, her amateur beginning soon blossomed into paid weekend gigs. Scouts often approached her about being in front of the camera, but Joy was comfortably at home behind it. So much so that she changed her minor from multimedia journalism to photography the second semester in school. However, she continued to pursue a bachelor's degree in communication.

"Have you said anything about it to your dad?" Tiana questioned.

"No," she slowly spoke, "You know Dad. He's cool with whatever I decide, as long as I'm doing something." She quietly chuckled. "And ever since Ma retired from the DA's office and began spending time with all of her grandchildren, she's mellowed out over the years."

Joy spoke of her growing group of nieces and nephews. In addition to ZJ and the triplets her brother, Zachary, and his wife, Bianca, shared, her other brother, Joshua, and his wife, Gayle, had two children of their own, a boy and girl each. Her sister, Elisha, doted over the two-year-old toddler she shared with her husband, Tyler. Gerald and Margaret reveled in having a guest house constructed on their sprawling property to accommodate the revolving visits from their children and grandchildren. Joy smiled at the thought of their expanding family. Especially since her sister, Charity, and husband, Milton, welcomed their first child, a baby girl, this past spring.

"I'm still going to use my degree, just in a different way. And besides, I'm making good money, my *own* money, and I haven't even graduated yet. That's got to count for something, right?"

"Look, I hear ya, girl. You don't have to convince me, but you have some explaining to do to your brother." Tiana smirked.

Joy shrugged as she stood and paced back and forth in front of the window. She stopped beside a family photo that rested on an end table. "Zachary knows me," she said, staring out of the window. "I kind of mentioned it to him the last time he was home. I don't think it'll be a big surprise." Joy looked back at her friend who she could clearly tell was quietly absorbing her words. "That's what it's all about, right? Finding our own way and making our own decisions as adults. I'm walking across that stage in the spring with a Bachelor of Arts degree, but my heart is really not in broadcasting or journalism anymore."

"You're really serious about ditching broadcasting all together for photography, huh?"

Joy looked at the wooden table that held a stack of business cards with her name printed on them. "I am," she confidently answered. "It's all going to work together for good."

"I hear you, putting Scripture on it." Tiana smiled. "God laid it down in Romans 8:28."

"It's the only way to go." Joy picked up one of the cards and held it in her hand. "God is already opening more doors."

"How so?" Tiana gathered the stacks of clothes she had folded and began carefully putting them back in the basket.

"Well, you heard about that short indie film being shot downtown, right?" Joy's face brightened.

"Yeah, the one that's going to have all those streets blocked off for a couple days," Tiana lamented. "As if traffic isn't going to be bad enough with classes starting again." She groaned as she grabbed one of the few pieces of clothing left to fold.

"Well, your girl has been hired to be a local set photographer."

"Are you serious?" Tiana's voice went up an octave as she leaned forward.

"*Yes*!" Joy nodded repetitively as smiles grew between them. "I just got the call this morning."

"Oh my goodness, things are really happening for you!" Tiana giggled with excitement as she wrinkled the pink cotton blend blouse tightly gripped in her hands. "You're not playing around."

"Not at all. And it couldn't have come at a better time." Joy's voice held hope. "But I'm going to need your help. I want somebody there with me to kind of feel things out since it'll be my first time working on a project like this. It doesn't pay much, but the experience could be huge."

"That's great. Your portfolio is going to be on point."

"I'm trying, girl. *So* ...will you come with me today? It's before classes start and you told me earlier that you don't have to work." Joy then put her hands in a praying position as she begged, "*Please, say yes...*"

"Oh, girl, I'm there!" Tiana appeared more excited than Joy as she bounced in place and hugged her friend. "You didn't even have to ask."

Chapter Three

OF ALL MORNINGS, HE picked today to dial her number. Joy ignored the call and let it go to voicemail. Rico had some nerve contacting her after the way he waltzed out of her life. She learned that he had lied about the landlord having his apartment renovated over the summer before classes restarted. It was just his way of weaseling into her home before he skipped town. She discovered that after the property management company called her about his last month's rent. He had cleverly listed her as a reference on his rental application.

A day after Rico left, Joy found yet another small baggie on the floor beside the Murphy bed in her office where he had slept. She had ignored the sense that something had become increasingly off about him and accepted him at face value. Joy blamed herself for losing thousands because of this man, money she had earned from photographing clients. Now she was tasked with the chore of cleaning her place top to bottom to make sure all his drugs were out of her home.

When Tiana asked her if it was really love, Joy understood that love didn't act that way. Nothing about how he treated her displayed characteristics of love. After hours of crying, the night Rico left, she tried to soothe the pain in her chest while questioning why she had ever let him into her life. Joy's tears weren't because of Rico's sudden departure. They stemmed from regret. When she told Tiana that she wasn't sad about him leaving, she was indeed telling the truth. In fact, his departure brought relief. It was the realization that he had used her that caused her pain and shame. It was hard enough for her to admit that she had been scammed by someone she cared about, but it was even more difficult to make this revelation known to her friends. Both Tiana and Michelle had voiced that they saw it coming. Joy supposed they saw things about her relationship that she didn't see for the same reason she had seen things in theirs that they couldn't.

Despite her limited dating history, from the handful of guys she had gone out with, this one hurt her on a different level. When Rico said he cared for her, she believed him, despite her misgivings. She relied on the words he spoke instead of the actions he showed. *Big mistake. Trust what the Bible says, you will know them by their fruits.*

Determined to move on, romantic relationships were out of the question ... at least until she finished college. Joy wanted to eliminate distractions and focus on finishing this phase of her life strong.

"Ready to go?" Tiana asked as she slipped into the straps of her backpack style purse. "Do you need me to carry anything?"

Joy smoothed the sides of her carefully coiffed hair that was in an attractive updo. She looked in the oval mirror hanging on her hallway wall and applied a thin layer of rose-tinted lip gloss. "If you could pull my roller bag out while I get my camera tote and wallet, that'd be great." She turned from the mirror and quickly grabbed the green smoothie she had blended just moments prior from the kitchen counter.

"Sure. I'll start the car and meet you outside." Tiana retrieved the roller bag and key to Joy's Acura. She walked out the door, but abruptly stopped as she nearly tipped over a glass vase in front of her. "Watch out!" Tiana held up her arm as Joy rushed out behind her.

"What in the world?" Joy glared at the bouquet of flowers on her doorstep. She gripped the smoothie's insulated tumbler in one hand and carefully picked up the vase with the other, examining the arrangement for a clue as to who sent them.

"Do you think it's Rico?" Tiana questioned.

"Not a chance." Joy shook her head. "He doesn't have any money."

"Then who? I don't have a boyfriend."

"I don't know, we'll figure it out later." Joy quickly took the vase back inside and carefully placed it on the kitchen counter. "Let's go." She raced back out, slamming the door shut behind them.

After a short drive through town, Joy checked in at the venue and took her place on set. It wasn't a major motion picture sound stage, but she was happy, nonetheless. Since she was familiar with video camera placement thanks to her brother, Zachary, Joy was empowered that she had managed to get hired as an independent contractor without any of her family's help. In high school, she was homecoming queen, student body president, and voted most likely to succeed. But deep inside she questioned whether it was due to her own gifts and talents or because of the notoriety of being a part of the Maxwell family pedigree.

The morning hours were a blur as she snapped frames of everything and every actor. She knew her camera angles and recognized where she should stand, just like a pro. By lunch, Joy's confidence was palpable. The uncertainty that led her to invite Tiana along had segued into the assurance she held when working with other clients. She was in her element.

"Do you see what I see?" Tiana whispered to Joy as she discreetly motioned with a slight nod toward the pizza food truck several yards away. "That cute white guy over there is checking you out."

The Caucasian twenty-nine-year-old male with a lean build and striking features gazed at the equally attractive African American twenty-one-year-old Joy Maxwell, who could easily pass for a fitness model. From a distance, the man's piercing blue eyes scaled Joy's athletic physique from head to toe. He gazed in admiration, barely noticing that he had missed his place in line to order a refill of organic lemon-iced green tea.

"Oh girl, please. You mean that guy across the street? He's not looking at me." Joy smirked and rolled her eyes. "He's probably trying to figure out where we managed to get these fruit slushies because the machine over there is out of order." Joy shook her clear plastic cup, causing the ice chips inside to rattle, before taking a long satisfying drink.

"Girl, you really think he's staring over here like he's lost something because of some slushy?" Tiana shifted her probing brown eyes between the two of them.

"Uh, yeah. It's ninety degrees in the shade out here." Joy slurped her drink through the oversized lime green straw. "And stop staring. He's going to think we're talking about him."

"But we are." Tiana giggled.

"No, *you* are." Joy shook her head and gazed in another direction. "I hope they wrap this scene soon because I am about to melt."

Over half the day had passed as the cast and crew enjoyed a short break. There was only one other day of outside shooting before it moved to a closed set indoors. Joy could not wait for that. She was not the sit-in-the-heat type of girl. She hated being outdoors in the summer sun. But the summer evenings and nights accompanied by a light breeze off Lake Lewiston back home in Mississippi were another thing.

"Well, if you don't need me right now, I'm going to stand in that store over there for a few minutes. Me and this heat are not getting along right now. I need a break from the break." Tiana fanned herself with a folded piece of paper and murmured, "I'll be back."

Not more than ten seconds after Tiana left her post at her friend's side, the handsome stranger strolled in Joy's direction. Joy looked behind her because surely, he wasn't coming to talk to her. She placed her drink beside her on the wooden bench where she sat and picked up her camera. Joy lowered her head as she pretended to search for something in her black leather canvas tote.

"Excuse me, miss." His voice was smooth and inviting, carrying with it a hint of confidence.

Joy slowly looked up from her bag and their eyes met. "Yes."

His captivating blue eyes gazed at her as if he was in a trance. "Hi, my name is Chase." He extended his hand in her direction and quietly asked, "Have we met before? You look so familiar."

Oh, he's dragging that old line out of cold storage, Joy thought. The mere words brought a telling smile to her face. After she pulled her hand from the camera bag and touched his, a faint rush of emotions swept over her. His grip was strong, powerful even, yet not overbearing. She was flattered to think he was flexing for her because when they shook hands, the muscles in his arm rippled with the subtle movements of his fingers. No rings. No tan lines. His teeth were a fresh-from-the-dentist white, encased in a smile that was sure to photograph well, even in the worst lighting.

"I look familiar?" Joy's eyes drifted away from his as she noticed that he held her hand longer than she was comfortable with. "I don't think we've met before." She surveyed her surroundings and slowly pulled her fingers away.

As Joy's manicured hands landed on her lap, Chase held a fixed gaze that was lost in her deep brown eyes. Abruptly, he cleared his throat and carefully took a small step backward. "Maybe I have you confused with someone else." And then, with a telling smirk, he asked, "Weren't you at the botanical garden in Victory Square last weekend for a maternity shoot?"

Joy tilted her head and narrowed her eyes. She was indeed in Victory Square at the botanical garden for a maternity shoot last weekend, but how did he know that?

"What did you say your name was again?" Joy studied the movements of his lean structure, analyzing his flirtatious body language. She glanced away from him to the producer and director across the street, wondering if he even belonged on set.

"Chase ... and I'm sorry." He withdrew his smile as he recognized her suspicion. "That must've sounded awful. My sister, Patricia, was the one who had her photos taken. I was her driver that day."

"Oh, Patricia Melrose. She's your sister?"

"Yeah." Chase nodded with a look of admiration in his eyes. "The photos you took of her were very nice. You have a great eye." He paused, briefly folding in his lips that wore a telling smile. "I was wondering if you would take some of me for a website I'm having redone."

"For a website, huh?" she skeptically questioned.

"Yes ... maybe we can discuss the details over coffee sometime." Careful to maintain a respectable distance, Chase inched closer as his eyes filled with hope.

Joy flipped through her memory bank, and not one image of him materialized in her mind.

"And you were at the shoot with Patricia the entire time that day?" she tried to verify, unsure if he was telling her the truth. *For all I know, he could be a stalker*, she thought.

"Yes, well, except for the few minutes when I left to pick up a package from the post office," he explained. "I was there most of the time on a park bench out of the way."

"Oh, I didn't see you there."

In a deepened tone, he responded with one eyebrow raised, "But I saw you," before he casually relaxed his hands in his front pockets.

Now that phrase freaked her out. *But I saw you...* Who says that to someone you don't know? Joy looked back at the store where Tiana had retreated to find her staring at them through a large glass window. Joy summoned her with a wave of her hand and quickly zipped her bag shut. As she avoided eye contact with Chase, Joy grabbed her watery drink from the bench and stood. As if on cue, the assistant director called the cast and crew back into position.

"I'm sorry, but I have to get back to work." She moved around him towards the large tree trunk centered in the square cutout in the paved sidewalk. As Tiana met her a few feet away, Joy glanced back at Chase who gently scratched the side of his head and walked away in the opposite direction.

"Hey, what were you two talking about? I saw how he rolled up on you as soon as I went inside." Tiana smiled and slipped on her sunglasses.

When she was sure that Chase was out of earshot, Joy filled Tiana in on her suspicions. "He knows a little bit too much about me."

"So, you think dude is stalking you?" Tiana questioned as she found Chase posted across the street engaged in a conversation with two sound engineers.

"I don't know. He told me that he was at the photo shoot I had last weekend, and now he's here at another job that I have." Joy grunted under her breath as she draped her camera strap across her neck. "What would you think if it were you?"

Tiana swayed with a soft smile emerging on her lips. "I don't know, it sounds kind of romantic to me. What if he's the one who left you those flowers?"

Joy nudged her on the arm, recalling how they almost tripped over the glass vase on the doorstep as they rushed out the door this morning. "That would be even worse."

"How so?" Tiana grimaced.

"That would mean that he knows where I live." She widened her eyes.

"Oh yeah, I see your point."

"You know what? As soon as we break for the day, I'm going to let the producer know about this."

"Are you sure that's necessary?" Tiana placed a hand on Joy's forearm as she began to move toward the actors who stood farther along the sidewalk. "I mean, you said so yourself, this job is only for a few weeks. I would wait it out and see if he shows up tomorrow. For all you know, he could've been hired to work on set too. According to you, the only thing that he's done is say that he saw you at his sister's photo shoot as he waited for her."

"But what about the flowers?" Joy raised her eyebrows. "And the fact that he's now here?"

"Flowers that came from who knows where. And as for him being here, that could just be a coincidence. If you're really that concerned about it, call his sister. I would just bring it up to her," Tiana suggested. "Has she paid you yet?"

"Yeah, she's paid me. As a matter of fact, she texted me this morning about doing a session for a good friend of hers. It's a surprise gift. I'm trying to build my clientele as much as I can before classes start." Joy found Chase in the crowd again. She adjusted her camera lens and discreetly snapped several frames of him. "I'll see her again in a couple of days."

"Well, there you go. That's a perfect opportunity to find out more about their family. I don't get the stalker vibe from him, but I could be wrong." Tiana glanced over to where Chase now stood. "I've been known to be wrong before."

"Yes, I know. We both have." Joy leaned against her friend and laughed, referencing their interesting dating history.

"You're probably just thinking the worst after what happened with Rico."

"Maybe." Joy lowered her camera and shrugged. "But one thing's for sure, I'm not going to make the same mistake twice."

Chapter Four

CHASE DROVE ONTO THE gated property of the Carlington estate. His eyes roamed from the puffy clouds and smoky gray sky to the land that had been in his family for generations. The nearly twelve hundred acres provided a place for the animals that his family bred, showcased, and sold for a living. It was a family business that Chase tolerated but wanted no part of.

After parking his convertible along the long winding tree-lined driveway, Chase stood beside his vehicle and instinctively measured the humidity in the air. Rain was on the way. He wanted to quickly remedy whatever his parents' problems were and get back home before the impending storm hit. When he got an urgent call from his mother just moments before his father phoned, Chase knew that his own business had to take the backseat once again to the Carlington enterprise. Even with several staff members employed under their tutelage, no one was competent enough to handle the business quite like family, according to his father.

"Your father is waiting for you in his office." Those words from his petite mother met him as soon as he rounded the corner just a few feet shy of the formal dining room. "He's in quite a tizzy since Grayson announced this morning that he's selling his share."

"But Uncle Grayson enjoys working with those horses. Why would he give it all up?" Chase questioned.

"Working with the horses is one thing," she began in a southern drawl, "and working with your father is another. Ever since Grayson left that private club of theirs, brothers or not, things haven't been the same between them since. Your father is bent on giving Grayson the marked-up charge he's demanding to avoid an outsider taking the share."

Chase parked his hands at his waist and shook his head. He walked toward the large picture window in the adjoining room and folded his arms. "Looks like Dad has a monopoly now. After Aunt Virginia jumped ship last year, there's nobody left."

"Except for you, Patricia, and Booker." She eyed him as she poured liquid from a glass bottle wrapped inside of a cloth. "You know how he wants you all to take over."

"Yeah, I know. Looks like he's already roped in Paul." Chase spoke of his brother-in-law, Patricia's husband. "I hear he's already securing contracts for Dad."

"Well, you know your father. He enjoys working with family. And since Paul's a lawyer, it only made sense that he came on board after marrying Pat." Lucille took a gulp from her brimming highball glass.

"More like it only made sense to have him under his thumb too," Chase mumbled.

Lucille slowly lowered her glass, momentarily pressing her lips together, swallowing the liquid in her mouth. "What'd you say, honey? I didn't hear you."

"Nothing." Chase's stare lingered on his mother as she sipped from her tall glass again. "Are y'all expecting company tonight?" His eyes shifted to the open liquor cabinet a few feet from where she stood.

"No, why do you ask?" She cleared her throat and placed the glass on the exquisitely carved dining table. She needless-ly adjusted the honeycomb designed runner where matching placemats flanked a stack of folded napkins.

"Never mind." He suspected that she was making her famous Alabama Bramble cocktail in the middle of the day again.

"Oh, you mean because I'm in the dining room. It's not what you think. Your father and I just decided to have lunch in here this afternoon since the room is barely used nowadays." Lucille gently smiled and hurried him along. "You better get on in there. He's expecting you."

"Yeah, I guess I better before he texts me again." Chase walked over to his mother and kissed her on the cheek. As he leaned close to her, his suspicions were confirmed. She smelled like a distillery. "Mom, is everything okay?"

"You're always worrying about me." She patted his hand that rested on her shoulder. "Everything is fine."

"Dad's not at it again, is he?"

"*Sshh,*" she abruptly shushed him. "Your father and I are fine now. That was a one-time thing and it's over. He's promised me and I believe him." Lucille spoke candidly of her husband's infidelity. Their marriage had hit a rough patch around the time Patricia graduated from college just over four years ago. Years had passed before Lucille learned of his adultery. Upon her discovery he ended things with the other woman and vowed to never do it again.

Chase reached around her and grabbed the bottle hidden behind the ice bucket on the bar cart in the corner of the room. "Are you sure?"

"Yes, I'm sure." Lucille took the bottle from his hand and placed it inside the liquor cabinet. She secured the doors and faced her son again. "I'm okay ... *we're* okay. I was just having a light cocktail like I've always had for the past twenty-five years. It's nothing like before. No need for you to worry." She patted his chest.

"I love you, Mom." Chase kissed his mother on the forehead as he hugged her. It wasn't easy for him to digest the fact that she had begun drinking after having him and his siblings.

"I love you too, Chase." She released his embrace and looked up into his eyes. "Don't tell your father about this. I don't want him going on about that Betty Ford Center again. I'm fine."

"We all just want what's best for you." Chase's face dripped with pity.

When Lucille found out about the woman his father had been fooling around with, she nearly had a nervous breakdown.

Her life revolved around him and the mere thought of losing their marriage was terrifying. The prenuptial agreement alone would leave her with nothing.

"Promise me, not a word to him. I'm still coping with Dinah's passing. Especially after missing her funeral and all." Lucille glanced at the scented candle on the glass pedestal in the corner. It was a gift Dinah had given to her one birthday. "Despite what your father thought of her, she was like family to me."

Chase nodded, remembering the housekeeper their family had employed for over thirty years. Dinah, alongside her husband, Leroy, who was the family's chauffeur, practically raised him and his siblings. In addition to weekly shuttles to the airport and periodic dinner parties for the Carlington household, rain or shine, Leroy transported Chase and his siblings to and from school, sporting events, and even sat in on a couple football games and ballet recitals that their parents were too busy to attend. The rotating fleet of luxury vehicles accommodated their lifestyle well and didn't hurt Leroy's image either.

"I miss her, too." Chase wore a nostalgic gaze, still trying to shake the image of her in that casket. "She was like a second mother to me."

It pained him to witness the way his father had treated the hardworking couple, simply because of the color of their skin. They were viewed as more of an asset than faithful employees. Workers who rarely asked for a day off and never complained about the growing list of job duties expected of them.

As Chase grew older, he began to understand why his mother would secretly send Dinah home with a covered basket of food for her waiting children. It was a special treat when his father worked out of town. Those were the times Lucille invited the couple's children over to play in the spacious backyard with Chase and his siblings. As the day drew into evening, Dinah and Leroy would sit down in the expansive dining room for a home-cooked meal Lucille had prepared herself.

"Mr. Leroy appreciated everything you did for her. Paying those medical bills and then for the funeral too."

"Well, I did what I could without hearing noise from your father," she grumbled. "He never paid them what they were worth when they worked here. After Dinah got sick and everything, Leroy didn't need to be worrying about bills and such. It was the least I could do."

Lucille and Chase both turned their attention to the chime coming from his phone. Chase pulled the cell out of his pocket and saw that it was a text from his father.

"He's asking where I am." Chase held the phone in his mother's direction. "I better get in there."

"Okay." Lucille carefully sat down in a chair at the table. "I think I'm going to lie down for a nap. It has been quite an afternoon. I was on the brink of a migraine." She let out a weary sigh and gently leaned her forehead against her hand. "If you hear from Booker, tell him I want to talk to him." She spoke of her eldest son. "He was supposed to help out with the dogs this week, but he's not answering his phone."

"Mom, don't stress yourself out about Booker or the dogs. It'll work out." Chase slid the phone back in his pocket. He touched her on the shoulder before starting in the opposite direction. "Talk to you later."

Chase walked away from his mother and toward his father's home office just down the hall. Before he ventured inside, Chase could hear his father on the office phone having a heated discussion. When he opened the French doors, Phillip Carlington, often referred to as Phil by most, motioned him inside. Chase cleared his throat as the pungent woodsy aroma infiltrated his nostrils. He left the door ajar to abate the cigar smoke in the room and patiently waited as Phil disputed a fraudulent charge on his credit card statement.

"This is the second time this month I've had to change my card number!" Phil growled out of frustration. "I've had better service from the burger joint downtown." With a heavy pound on the large desk in front of him, Phil stood his ground on a purchase he was adamant that he did not make.

Chase sighed to himself and gripped the top of the round back chair parked in front of the desk. He repetitively tapped the top of the chair with his fingers while waiting for his father's conversation to end. Moments later, Phil slammed the phone onto the base and grunted.

"Hey, son, good to see you." Phil motioned for Chase to sit down and picked up the cigar he had temporarily abandoned while on the phone.

"Dad," Chase curtly replied with a slight nod as he reluctantly sat in the chair across from him. He refrained from inquiring about the recent phone call, wanting this visit to be short so that he could get back to work on his own projects.

"I called you over here because I'm gonna need your help this weekend. I had to fire a stable hand yesterday and some of the others decided they wanted to leave, too. So, here we are running a skeleton crew for the trainers when we've got to get those horses ready for the upcoming shows." Phil rubbed his full jaw as he spoke of the equestrian dressage shows. "And remember, it's *your* racehorse taking up some of my workers' time," he pointed out, "but I will say that she's also the most promising on this year's circuit."

The three horses Chase was bequeathed from his grandfather, one of which was foaled by a prize-winning thoroughbred, proved to be a lucrative investment in the race circuit over the past year.

"See if you can call around and get some bodies over here like yesterday. Your mother is on the brink of a conniption, drinking again, and I've got meetings coming out of the wazoo." Phil thumbed through a stack of papers as he rambled on. "I've got contracts to read, so I need you to come through for me on this one, son."

"Dad, I have a business of my own to run." Chase squared off as he rose from the chair. "And for the record, I take care of my own horses, and Impartially True has her own trainer."

"On *my* land," Phil said, matching the stench of his son's tone.

Chase stared as his father dumped a heap of ashes from his cigar into a waiting ash tray on his desk. Things had been strained between him and his father for a while now. Ever since he broke away from the family business to handle his own, Phil stubbornly held it against him. Chase had no issues with the industry itself, but ever since his grandfather's sudden passing a few years ago, he struggled to find common ground with his father who was now in charge.

"And sit down while I'm talking to you," Phil instructed, pointing at the chair his son had abandoned.

Chase glared at him but reluctantly obeyed.

"I don't ask too much of you these days, and I wouldn't ask at all if I didn't need you." Phil folded his arms across his chest.

"Can't you ask Booker?" Chase questioned, offering up his older brother.

"Now you know good and well he's a prodigal." His southern drawl thickened. "The only thing I can rely on your brother to do is nothing. I'm still trying to straighten out that mess he left me with last month. No, you're the only one I can rely on." He pointed his chubby fingers at him. "Patricia can't do it right now, so it's got to be you." He looked over the brim of his glasses with furrowed brows and glared at Chase. "Remember, son, you owe me one."

How could he forget? Phil brought it up every chance he got. After all the favors he'd done for his father, none of them ever evened the score in Phil's book. While Chase had the privilege of purchasing a luxuriously customized dream home with the generous inheritance from his late grandfather and funding the capital needed for his business, he still relied on his father's help to catapult his company into a competitive corporation. The connections to high profile consumers that Phil linked him to were always being held over his head. Chase had since formed many business relationships on his own, but the more Phil revived the issue, the more resolved he became to buy him out as an early investor and cut those ties with his father.

"So, is that a yes? All I need is a few days from you to square things with the vendors and coordinate transportation for the horses. Once that's settled, we'll fare out. Dakota and Bryce will be back from vacation, and you can get back to your little startup."

"Dad, it's not a startup anymore. We grossed well into seven-figures last year."

"That's good, but what about all that overhead you've got? Employees, inventory, and the miscellaneous things." Phil released a throaty laugh. "All you need is right here on the ranch, but you chose carpentry. Come back when you've crossed the eight-figure threshold of profitability, then maybe I'll stop calling it a startup." His gross arrogance reeked in the room.

Chase grunted under his breath, knowing that his father was still miffed at him for not staying in the family business of horse training, riding lessons, and equestrian dressage. The breeding of pure dog pedigree and occasional dog shows had also contributed to their financial success. At every turn, Phil degraded the seriousness of Chase's growing furniture business. The disparaging words of his father did not deter him, though, but rather provided fuel for motivation.

"Maybe you can start with Leroy's boy. I know they need money since their momma's passing. He came around looking for work a few days ago. Don't let him know we need him. Make it look like we're doing him a favor."

"Dad, he's not a boy." A look of disgust spilled across Chase's face. "He's older than I am."

"He's a boy to me," he sternly responded. "Maybe he has some friends that want to make a little money too. Don't make grand promises." Phil eyed his son as he added, "Keep the budget tight."

Chase grunted under his breath and shook his head. "Anything else?"

Phil sucked in a pocket of air from his cigar and released a plume of smoke from his mouth. "No."

When Chase turned around, his eyes were immediately drawn to the relic on the wall above the French doors. He stared for a moment before glaring back at his father.

"Do you like it? I had it framed and hung last week." Phil stood and proudly grinned at his treasured possession.

At that moment, Chase flinched from the jolting clap of thunder. "I better get going before the weather gets too bad." He stared back at the Confederate flag tucked behind a thick sheet of glass encased in a wooden frame, tightened his jaw, and walked out the door.

Chapter Five

"I'LL CALL YOU BACK later. I'm here now," Joy said as she ended a call with Michelle. She popped her trunk and got out of her vehicle. The inclement weather yesterday almost caused her to call last night and cancel today's shoot, but she was glad that she hadn't as the storm quickly passed over.

"Joy, I'm glad you found the place alright!" Patricia waved her hand as she stood from the white rocking chair on her front porch. "Do you need any help?"

With a gentle smile, Joy waved back and responded, "Oh, no. I'm good. I only have a couple of things to bring inside." She gathered her items from the trunk and temporarily rested them on the paved driveway. "You gave great directions. Better than the GPS on my phone, I'll tell you that."

"I don't know why, but it always tries to send people on a back road that no longer exists." Patricia held her front door open for Joy to enter. "Thanks again for coming on such short notice. My friend is already here in the back room getting dolled up. We had our nails and toes done earlier." She wiggled her fingers in Joy's direction, proudly showing off her pink nails. "I just decided to make a day of it, you know. After losing all that weight, I just wanted her to know that she is appreciated. Bariatric surgery or not, she put in some hard work."

"That is so nice. I'm sure she's loving you for this." Once inside, Joy moved her sunglasses from her eyes to the top of her head. "Just point in the direction where you want me to set up. Indoor, outdoor, or a mixture of both?"

"Um, I think you should probably do both." Patricia patted her forehead with a handkerchief from the pocket of her colorful print maxi maternity dress. "I don't have a view like Victory Square, but I'm sure Sandy will love it just the same."

Joy's eyes drifted around the room, taking in the elegant décor. The hand-carved pieces she focused on reminded her of the vases and candle holders she had recently purchased this past spring. She examined the natural lighting of a few rooms as she scanned areas of the partially open floor plan design. When she recognized Chase in a framed photo among a wall filled with other wedding pictures just off the drawing room, Joy's gaze lingered.

"I like the black and white prints." Joy pointed at the strategic placements on the wall. "Your wedding photographer did a great job."

"Oh, thank you. I just love vintage photos, but it was more of my brother's idea than mine. He said that it gives a classic look. So, I had his specially developed in black and white, a couple in sepia too. Those are the ones where he really looks like our grandfather."

"Your brother?" Joy raised an eyebrow, eager to confirm that she was indeed related to the mysterious stranger she had met on set.

"Yes, this is my brother Chase." Patricia pointed at the attractive man whose profile filled the frame. "And over here is my other brother, Booker," she mentioned, gesturing to a neighboring photo.

"Do you have any sisters-in-law?" Joy cleverly asked.

"No, not yet. I was the first out of the three of us to get married. And I'll be the first to give my parents a grandchild." She smiled and gently patted her stomach.

Joy nodded. "Oh, okay." At least now she knew that Chase didn't have any children running around. "You mentioned at our last session that you work in the family business. Do your brothers work in the business as well?"

"Well, sort of." Patricia smiled. "My oldest brother, Booker, comes and goes. And Chase, the middle one, is striking out on his own."

"What do you mean striking out on his own?" Joy's curiosity grew. "What does he do?"

"He's a carpenter," Patricia answered.

A carpenter, Joy thought. "Really?" She looked at Patricia in surprise.

"Well, not everyone is cut out to work with animals day in and day out," Patricia chuckled, "but that's what us Carlingtons do." She proudly referenced the lineage of her father's family that dated back over a century.

Carlington ... so that's his last name. Joy softly smiled.

"Even my husband has come aboard." Patricia spoke fondly of Paul. "This little bundle of ours will be a Melrose." She cradled her belly in her hands again. "But I'm sure he or she will follow in my family's footsteps just the same."

Joy glanced at the photo of Chase again before following Patricia into another room. "Well, you have a beautiful home." Patricia guided her past the kitchen of the open-concept house through the glass sliding door that led to the attractively decorated four-seasons room. "I really like how the sun sets just beyond the skyline of trees. What a way to unwind at the end of a long day."

"Thank you for your kind words, but I can't take credit for the view." Patricia casually touched Joy on the shoulder and chuckled softly. "That's all God."

"That is true." Joy's demeanor brightened at the mention of God. "Isn't He amazing though?"

"Yes, He is." Patricia cleared her laptop and a book from the wrought iron table in the corner of the expansive sunroom.

"Were you raised in church?" Joy inquired as she opened her roller bag. She split her attention between Patricia and the props she brought for the gifted photo shoot.

"Not exactly." Patricia placed one of her hands on the small of her back as she eased into a cushioned seat. "My parents weren't spiritual people, but the friend who's having the session with you today invited me to Vacation Bible School one summer."

"Is that how you came to know Jesus?" Joy asked as she adjusted the portrait background screen she had just pulled from its case.

"It changed my life forever," Patricia confessed. "I mean, I'd heard of God before, especially from my grandparents on my dad's side, but the church where my friend, Sandy, attended was just different."

"How so?" Joy questioned.

"It was the first church I had gone to that had just about every race of humanity in it." With a reflective gaze, it appeared as though Patricia had been transported to the past. "They were big on making everyone feel welcome, regardless of their background. The pastor always said that he wanted the church to look like Heaven. No segregation there." Patricia paused and released a heavy sigh. "To be completely transparent, we were raised to not be unequally yoked."

Joy's forehead wrinkled at her statement. "Aren't all Christians supposed to not be unequally yoked?"

Patricia cautiously shook her head. "Not the way we were raised. They taught us that races shouldn't mix. That we aren't equals."

"*What*?" Joy glared at her, stunned by her remark.

"But that's not what I believe now," Patricia quickly clarified, becoming more careful with her words. "Trust me, I know that the Bible teaches we are not to be unequally yoked *with unbe-*

lievers. I understand now that was only a portion of Scripture people used to justify their lifestyle."

"Oh ... okay." Joy fell silent.

Here she was in a white woman's house who had just confessed that her family raised her to think that white supremacy was okay. Although Patricia had expressed that she no longer shared those views, Joy's guard went up. And she wondered if Chase, somewhere deep inside, harbored those beliefs his sister now professed to be of the past.

"I'm sorry." Patricia disrupted the awkward break of silence as her eyelids fluttered. "I have a tendency to ramble. You asked about how I became a Christian and I just felt comfortable sharing. I hope that's okay." She gently placed a hand on Joy's arm.

"Sure," Joy slowly answered. She then forced a smile. "I'm glad you feel comfortable talking to me. Like you said, that was the past."

"Yes, it is." Patricia eagerly nodded. She touched the front of her neck and quietly cleared her throat. "Would you like something to drink?"

Joy shook her head. "No, I'm good."

"Okay." Patricia nodded as she carefully rose from the chair. "Please excuse me for a moment. I'm going to let Sandy know you're here and use the restroom. Do you need anything?"

Joy shook her head, glancing at her camera and the props she had removed from her bag. "No, I have everything I need."

Just then, Paul poked his head out from behind the sliding glass door that led from the living room. He acknowledged Joy by holding up a hand to her before turning to his wife.

"Honey, I have a few things to finish up before heading to the office." Paul kissed Patricia on the cheek as she leaned slightly in his direction.

"Okay, I'll have dinner ready later. Just let me know when you finish up," Patricia replied.

"Oh, that's right. Joan started her vacation today." He rested his hand against his forehead. "You don't have to cook. I can pick something up for us on the way back."

"That'd be nice." Patricia smiled at Paul. "I'll walk with you to your car. Just let me use the restroom first." She looked at Joy again as she stood in the doorway. "I won't be long."

Joy nodded and watched as the couple retreated through the sliding door that led back into the main living area of the home. With a soft exhale, she turned around and soaked in the scenery.

The poolside was an oasis retreat. The intricate attention to detail was unparalleled. It sparked ideas in her mind about the additions her parents were making to their backyard. Their plans included a new guesthouse, an updated grilling area, and an in-ground pool. Joy captured a few pictures of Patricia's outdoor living space to share with her mother.

You never finished telling me about the flowers. Was it him? You can't leave me hanging like that, Michelle texted Joy.

Observing the now vacant door that Patricia and Paul had occupied just moments before, Joy quickly dialed Michelle's number. The call went to voicemail, so she hung up and walked to the large picture window and stared at the incredible view. Just as she started to venture beyond the sunroom to the patio and poolside, Michelle called her back.

"Are you done already?" Michelle asked.

"No, I'm not done. I haven't even gotten started yet. She's still getting ready." Joy glanced at the vacant door again before turning back towards the pool. "But I have a few minutes."

"You know the suspense is getting to me." Michelle chuckled. "I don't know why you started telling me about that guy right before getting off the phone."

"You were the one that was too busy to talk earlier." Joy giggled at her friend's relentless curiosity.

"Girl, have you forgotten that I have a two-year-old? Anyway, what happened?"

"Okay, okay. I'll give you the shortened version." Joy attempted to fill Michelle in on the flowers delivered to her home. She surmised that it was Chase because in all the time she had spent with Rico, not once did he have flowers delivered to her.

"And you said his name is Chase?"

"Yes. Chase Carlington."

"So, this guy found out where you lived and just up and sent flowers to you?"

"Girl, yes. I mean, what was he thinking? You can't be sending flowers to a black woman's house that you don't know."

"Not too many white women are fond of it either," Patricia interjected as she walked up behind Joy.

Joy quietly gasped as she turned and faced Patricia. "Michelle, let me call you back," she said into the phone before lowering it to her side. She stared with apologies etched on her face and sighed. "I'm sorry about that."

Patricia placed three chilled bottles of water on the table alongside her checkbook. "So, you know my brother? Is that why you were asking questions about him back there?" She tilted her head slightly and folded her arms across her chest. "Just be straight with me."

Joy briefly lowered her eyes to the floor before staring Patricia in the eyes. "Okay. I didn't want to mention it, but I met him earlier this week on another job. He approached me saying that he saw me at the park in Victory Square when I had a session with you. He said that the pictures were nice and—"

"And he asked you out." Patricia chuckled.

Joy's forehead wrinkled. "How did you know?"

"Well, that day on the way home, he told me that he wanted to send a thank-you note for how well you took care of me." Patricia easily smiled as she shook her head. "I'm sorry ... I gave him your address. I know we exchanged information so that we could get together some time in the future, but I didn't think he was going to send flowers too."

A thank-you note? Joy wondered.

"I was a little emotional earlier that day and you calmed my nerves. Chase has always been protective of me. Even at twenty-nine years old, he sometimes still acts as if I need a bodyguard. And I'm a married woman now." The sound of her soft laughter filled the air before gradually giving way to a more serious tone in her voice. "He just wanted to express his gratitude. I should have known better than to give him your address. Especially when he rambled on about how beautiful you are."

"He thinks I'm beautiful?" Joy visibly processed the information. The flutter of her eyelashes to the subtle rise of the corners of her mouth was revealing. "He said that to you?"

Patricia noticed when Joy blushed. It was clear to her that Joy had a mutual spark of interest in him too. "He's going to get me for this, but yes, that is what he said. And just so you know, he doesn't randomly hand out compliments like that."

Upon hearing those words, Joy unsuccessfully concealed her hidden attraction to Chase. When he spoke to her a couple days prior, his approach was met with a mixture of apprehension and other unspoken emotions. However, it didn't eliminate her lingering curiosity. Joy had to admit to herself that because he was white, she was hesitant to express her attraction towards him. She had never dated outside of her race, and the opinions of what others might think of the two of them together made the possibility a fleeting thought.

"Oh, I'm sorry about how that phone call must've sounded earlier." Joy shook her head, mirroring the same embarrassment that Patricia had shown when she disclosed her and Chase's upbringing.

"No need to be sorry, I get it." Patricia shrugged and then waved it off. "My brother is a hopeless romantic."

Joy's interest was piqued. "Is he always like this?"

"No, nothing like that. It's just that he ... hmm, how can I say this?" Patricia looked off to the side as she momentarily folded in her lips. "Wears his heart on his sleeve. Just know that he doesn't mean any harm. If he had, I would be the first to tell you." She then handed over a check.

Joy stared at the amount and then met eyes with her again. "This isn't what we agreed on."

"I know." Patricia smiled and lightly touched Joy's arm. "I think your services are worth a lot more than what you charge. Consider it a bonus."

Joy smiled warmly in return, surprised at the generous bonus.

"And you may as well expect to be busier this fall. When I have my baby shower and everyone sees the maternity album you're designing, I'm sure all of my friends will want to know about the eye behind the camera. Not to mention how I'm sure you'll memorialize Sandy's weight loss."

Joy's heart flushed with excitement and anticipation of things to come. "Speaking of your friend, when will I get to meet her?"

"I tried to check on her when I went inside, but she wouldn't let me in the room. It's like she's getting married or something." Patricia chuckled.

"This is a pretty big deal for her, huh?" Joy grinned.

"Like you wouldn't believe. I'm grateful that I can do this for her. Now, I'm counting on you to make her look like a movie star," Patricia teased, playfully pointing at Joy.

"No pressure," Joy responded with a chuckle. She then gestured to their surroundings. "With a view like this, we can't go wrong, right?"

"Right," Patricia agreed.

"I'm ready!" Sandy waved after she suddenly appeared at the glass door.

Joy and Patricia turned their attention to her with growing smiles on their faces.

"How do I look?" she asked, completing a graceful pirouette in a stunning yellow halter dress with a flowing, soft flare hem.

"Oh my goodness, look at you!" Patricia walked towards her and carefully held Sandy's arms open. She gently touched the soft curls of her friend's brunette hair, making note of the new caramel highlights. "You look great."

"Thank you." Sandy was absolutely giddy. "I can hardly believe how I look." She caught her reflection in the mirror Joy had set up in the corner of the room.

"Well, you have worked very hard, so enjoy the payoff." Patricia looked at Joy and gently edged Sandy in her direction. "This is Ms. Maxwell, your photographer for the evening. She is going to take good care of you."

"Nice to meet you." Joy extended her hand. "And call me Joy."

"It's nice to meet you too." Sandy smiled in return as she shook Joy's hand. "I'm Cassandra, but everybody calls me Sandy."

Patricia sipped from her water bottle and rested in a lounge chair out of the camera view as Joy attractively arranged the locks of Sandy's hair across her shoulders. She watched as Joy captured flattering frames of her friend in various poses against multiple backdrops. Sandy presented like a professional with Joy's direction. It hadn't taken Patricia long to dub Joy as her personal photographer. She was reliable, relatable, and easy to talk to.

"What do you think so far, Sandy?" Joy angled the digital screen of her camera towards Sandy that displayed pictures of her. "If you approve, we can get some pictures of you outside."

"Oh my goodness, they're beautiful!" Sandy exclaimed. She cupped her hands over her mouth as her eyes drifted to Patricia in surprise.

"Let me see." Patricia sat up in her chair as Joy angled the small screen in her direction. "Aww, yes, they are beautiful. I cannot wait to see them in print."

"Me either!" Sandy bounced in place as Joy nodded with a slight smile before she gathered a few props for the next set of pictures near the pool.

Patricia grinned as she reached for the buzzing cell on the glass table. After she silenced an incoming call from her father, Phil, she quietly exhaled as her fixed gaze on the phone dimmed. Her eyes briefly drifted to the pool area where the sound of laughter echoed in the distance, before she looked back at her phone. Patricia watched as the screen slowly faded to black, her disappointment evident as she shook her head.

Joy was an intelligent, beautiful woman – inside and out – but she was black. Phil's deeply held racial beliefs, distorted by misquoted passages of the Bible, often led to brazen outbursts. No matter how often Patricia tried to get Phil to understand the Scriptures as written, he would debate with her at every turn. After a while, Patricia surrendered it to God in prayer. There she realized that she was not responsible for a true conversion in her father. She was only called to plant and water seeds of faith. It was only the Holy Spirit Who could make it grow.

After discovering Joy's mutual interest in Chase, Patricia softly whispered to herself, "I'm going to add them to my prayer list too."

Chapter Six

"HE'S AN INVESTOR IN the film!" Joy shrieked as she flipped on the overhead lights to Tiana's bedroom and rushed to her side.

"What?" Tiana shielded her face from the blinding light with the back of her hand. "What time is it?"

"Eight o'clock," Joy spouted, holding a tablet in her hand. "He probably thinks I'm the crazy one." Her face was flushed with excitement as she scrolled through the screenshots saved on the device. They were captured from an article posted months prior about the production where she now worked.

It had been three days since Joy had seen Chase, and oddly enough, she couldn't get him off her mind. Since he hadn't shown up since that first day on set, she began sleuthing online. Joy began with social media searches that went nowhere as she didn't have his last name at the time, but after being armed with the Carlington identifier, a treasure trove of information about their family materialized at her fingertips.

"Girl, I just got to bed at five. I've got to get some sleep before work." Tiana groaned, wanting to be well rested when she started her weekend shift later in the administrative office at a local dialysis clinic. "Show it to me later."

"Alright, alright." Joy slowly rose from the edge of Tiana's bed. "Go back to sleep. I'll show it to you when you get up." She playfully nudged her shoulder.

Tiana yawned and turned her back as she snuggled beneath the soft microfiber sheet. Joy turned the light off and quietly closed the bedroom door. She walked into the kitchen and placed her tablet on the marble countertop near a mountain of unopened mail. Joy had just gone through a stack the morning before, so she figured Tiana must've retrieved a fresh batch from the mailbox late last night.

There it was again, another reminder of her recent past: a postcard from Rico. Joy took the card and ripped it in half. It wasn't enough that she had blocked him from her phone and on social media, but now she wondered if she had to block him from sending her mail. She sucked her teeth and began preparing her morning meal.

Although fresh out of a horrible relationship with Rico, she flirted with the idea of a coffee date with Chase just as he had shamelessly flirted with her when they met. *No, I'm not even going to go there.* Joy dismissed the thought. She was firm in her decision to focus on finishing her senior year strong without any distractions. She wanted to grow her business and figure out what else she wanted to do after graduation. Distractions were definitely not a part of the plan. *But he's cute...* Joy's preoccupation with Chase had already caused a diversion long enough for her to burn the waffles in the toaster.

"*Oh no*," she mumbled, glaring down at the charred waffles that were the last two in the plastic bag she had fished out of a sea of packaged meals in her freezer.

Joy tossed her ruined breakfast, reminiscent of black hockey pucks, into the garbage and opted for a healthier choice of fruit salad and lightly buttered cinnamon raisin toast instead. She chased the simple meal with a chilled glass of lemon-infused water. With a few minutes to spare before she needed to log on for a video call with her sisters about a surprise dinner they were planning for their parents, Joy pulled the website up again where she had found Chase's luxury furniture company.

The Lord your God will make you abound in all the work of your hand... Deuteronomy 30:9

My Lord and Savior, Jesus Christ, was a carpenter, and with this noble profession comes diligent work. Whether you're looking for a custom piece or gallery staple, my team and I are ready to assist in bringing your dream home space up to your standards. Visit us today.

-Chase Carlington

After Joy perused his site, she discovered that the prized pieces she now possessed, previously purchased from a boutique outlet store near the capital city, had come from his namesake: Carlington Home Furnishings.

He really does need a new headshot, she thought as she stared at the screen, considering Chase's proposal of a photography session. *This one doesn't do him justice*. She touched the screen with her fingers and sighed. The last thing she needed was another relationship. Remembering the way Chase held her hand when he had asked her out for coffee, Joy knew it wasn't just about a photo shoot. After understanding his intention behind the flowers he had sent to her home, her curiosity was further aroused.

When she learned that the flowers were simply a thank-you for how well she took care of his sister during their session together, Joy's perception of him immediately changed. As Patricia explained, she was excited, but also incredibly nervous about the upcoming birth of her first child. The photographer she had originally scheduled, the one who had photographed her wedding, unexpectedly relocated to another state. That, in and of itself, added another layer of stress to Patricia's maternity plans. When she saw Joy's ad online and the polished portfolio displayed on her website, Patricia eagerly contacted her.

The conversation Joy had with her about the recent influx of nieces and nephews in her family, and the love between them, helped Patricia's anxiety subside. It was an especially nice touch when Joy included a list of Scriptures, ones that spoke of mothers in the Bible, as a backdrop to Patricia's reimagined ultrasound pictures. Joy gently smiled at the kind gesture of Chase's floral arrangement, now realizing that it was sent before he even knew she was a subcontractor on set. He was not the stalker she had initially thought he was. Rather, their meeting on the film set seemed to be a divine appointment.

The card meant to be delivered with the flowers he had sent her was unknowingly detached from the bouquet. When it was retrieved after the delivery van had been detailed by the cleaning crew, the company reissued the engraved silk laminated card with a fresh bouquet as an apology. Especially after the new employee hadn't followed protocol by getting someone to sign for the flowers.

Since Chase hadn't returned to the set, Joy scribbled down the address to his furniture store located on the outskirts of the city to personally thank him. She glanced at the clock and closed out the tab to his website. She adjusted her tablet on the dining table and pulled up her email. She clicked on the meeting link to connect with Elisha and Charity for their scheduled video call.

Gerald and Margaret's milestone wedding anniversary was readily approaching, and the siblings wanted to celebrate their parents in style with an intimate surprise party. Even with their somewhat unpredictable schedules, both Zachary and Joshua promised that they would try to make it back home for the quiet dinner party celebration with just their immediate family. With Joshua's recent retirement from professional football, not only was he still quite occupied with the string of real estate investments in his growing portfolio, he was also busy with his children whom he wanted to spend more time with. In his own words at the retirement party held for him, he said with a proud smile, "It's just time."

Originally Elisha's idea, Charity and Joy signed on with no objections to the proposed date in early October. Joy would be on fall break from school and Charity would be visiting to pick out a plot of land for her and Milton's future home. His time in the military was drawing to a close and retirement was on the horizon for him too. Being that Elisha lived only twenty minutes from their parents in Lewiston Springs, she tasked herself with coordinating and hosting the event at her and Tyler's new home under the guise of a housewarming.

"Hey, girl!" Elisha waved at Joy. "You are a hard woman to catch up with." She smirked, playfully pointing at her.

"I know." Joy laughed. "I have been super busy this week getting things together. You know how it is senior year."

"That I do. I'm so proud of you, sis. I've already told you that if you need anything, let me know. We're all rooting for you to finish strong." Elisha reached out to her toddler son, Jaxon, as he walked into view. "He is too." She waved his hand at Joy.

"I will and I know you all are." Joy waved at Jaxon as she saw Tyler enter the screen.

"Hey, sis!" Tyler raised a hand at Joy.

"Hey, bro!" She waved back just before he kissed Elisha on the cheek and told her that he was leaving for a few hours with their son. Joy watched as he handed her a plate of food and took Jaxon by the hand. "Father and son outing?" Joy asked Elisha as they walked out of the room.

"And grandfather," Elisha added with a smile as she pulled her hair up into a ponytail. "They're meeting Dad for breakfast and a few rounds of putt-putt golf."

"Let me guess, so you can get the day off."

"Yep." Elisha giggled, squirting hand sanitizer into the palm of her hand.

"I knew it." Joy smiled as she pulled a notepad towards her and grabbed an ink pen from a nearby holder. "So, how late is Charity going to be this time?"

"She texted not too long ago, saying that she overslept. Hold on." Elisha raised her forefinger and closed her eyes. She quickly said a prayer over her food and then pulled the plate closer that Tyler had placed in front of her. "I'm cutting her some slack because I know what it's like to have a little baby. And for her, living on a military base is taking some getting used to."

"I heard." Joy rolled her eyes and shrugged. "The new commander doesn't allow head scarves in the gym nor sunglasses in the commissary."

"And with the transitional lens on her new eyeglasses, she found out the hard way." Elisha rolled her eyes as she picked up her fork.

"She's always saying how Milton is the one in the military, not her." Joy sighed. "His retirement date can't get here fast enough for her. Just a few more months and she'll be moving home."

"Yeah, I'll be here to help her get things set up before Milton's official separation date next year. With his new intelligence job lined up, it's going to be nice having them close by." Elisha adjusted her computer screen with a paper towel.

"I know, and then the both of you can take road trips to see me." Joy winked at her sister. "Because I'm not trying to move back to Lewiston any time soon."

"We'll come see you." Elisha chuckled before taking in a forkful of the perfectly seasoned southwestern omelet.

Suddenly, Charity appeared on the screen. "I'm sorry to keep you guys waiting. Zoe is so fussy since she's been teething."

"Hey girly, let me see her." Joy leaned closer to the screen as if that would give her a better view of the baby in her sister's arms.

Charity turned Zoe's face to the camera as the baby relentlessly chewed on the chilled teething ring tightly gripped between her tiny fingers.

"*Aww...* she has gotten so big since last time I saw her." Joy gushed over her curly-haired niece with plump rosy cheeks. "I want to hold her."

"Well, you'll get a chance to in a couple months." Charity rested the fidgety baby against her chest and patted her back.

"I, for one, am ready to see my little niece in person." Elisha carefully pressed a napkin against her wet lips to absorb the remnant of hot tea she had just sipped from her Principal of the Year mug. "What time is Ma leaving there again?"

"Milton is on his way back from the airport. He should be here any time now. They left about thirty minutes ago." Charity wiped Zoe's mouth with a thick burp cloth after she released a heavy belch.

Joy giggled. "That's what was wrong with her. She just needed to let that out."

"Yeah, I think so. She just had her morning bottle." Charity smiled, caressing Zoe's back. "Oh, Elisha, I sent a little something for Jaxon back with Ma. I'm sorry I didn't get to mail it in time for his birthday."

"Oh, girl, I understand. You have your hands full right now." Elisha pointed at Zoe. "No problem. Hopefully, you got some rest while Ma was there."

"Some," Charity answered while pointing at her eyes. "One set of the bags are gone. I just need to get rid of this carry-on."

Both sisters laughed at Charity.

"Joy, just you wait." Charity removed the drowsy Zoe from her chest and carefully placed her in the bassinet beside her. "When it's your turn, you'll understand."

"She sure will. Married life comes with all kinds of changes," Elisha quipped. "But it is such a good thing."

"Great, in fact," Charity interjected.

"Just marry your best friend," Elisha added. "The beauty of it all is something else."

"Hey, you guys, I'm twenty-one *and* single. I'm not trying to get married right now. And babies? *Puh-lease.* Can I finish school first?"

This time, Elisha and Charity laughed at Joy's outburst.

"We know, nobody's trying to push you into anything. We were just saying." Elisha grinned as she began nibbling on a slice of crispy bacon.

"And please, take your time," Charity said in a quieter voice this time when she saw Zoe's eyes close.

"Yeah, what she said," Elisha added, shielding her mouth as she chewed.

"Of course," Joy answered, turning her attention to the engraved card on the table next to her.

"So, Charity, is Ma's flight supposed to get here later this afternoon?" Elisha asked. "She texted me last night about changing the time, but I wasn't sure if she had a layover or not."

"No layovers. She got a direct flight," Charity slowly answered. "I really hated to see her go. She was such a big help this summer."

"Tell me about it. When Jaxon was born, I was praising God for the help. If it wasn't for Mama, I don't know what I would have done. When I went back to work, her new design business took a back seat until he was sleeping through the night."

Joy halfway listened as her sisters chatted about the upcoming surprise dinner for their parents. She propped her face against her hand and vaguely paid attention as they talked through details of a catered four-course meal to be served by white-gloved waiters. Joy's thoughts drifted to what Chase might be doing at that very moment. She wondered if he had special hobbies that they might have in common. She even speculated about the kinds of foods he liked. *Does he eat soul food? Can he skate? Is he as chivalrous as Patricia made him out to be?*

"*Joy?*" Both Elisha and Charity called her name.

"Huh?" Joy snapped from her haze. "What?"

"We've called your name twice." Elisha squinted at her.

"I'm sorry." Joy sat up from her slumped position. "My mind was somewhere else."

Suddenly, Zoe cooed.

"Is she already asleep?" Joy asked, diverting attention from herself. "Wow, that didn't take long."

"Well, that's my cue. When she sleeps, *I* sleep." Charity yawned. "Keep me posted about everything. Talk to you guys later."

Joy and Elisha waved back as Charity logged off.

"It was good seeing you, lil sis. Will you be home Labor Day weekend?" Elisha polished off her meal and wiped her hands clean.

"Oh yes, definitely. I can't wait for Dad's barbeque." Joy rubbed her hands together. "I missed out Fourth of July, but I'll be there next month. And I get to spend some time with Jaxon."

"That sounds good … *So*, what are you doing today?" Elisha questioned, peering at her sister's background, seemingly searching Joy's home for clues.

"You know me, a little of this and a little of that," Joy answered, careful to keep her newfound interest a secret.

"So, no hot dates?" Elisha abruptly asked as she stared Joy square in the eyes, erasing the dazed look from her youngest sister's face.

"No, no dates," Joy replied with a flat tone, her voice lacking any hint of enthusiasm.

"Well, those flowers came from somewhere." Elisha pointed to the arrangement in the vase on the counter behind her sister.

"Oh, those?" Joy glanced back at the flowers as if it was the first time she had seen them. "It was just from this guy."

Joy avoided eye contact and fidgeted with the notepad where she had scribbled Chase's business address. It was harder to mask her emotions on video than over the phone.

"I know you, Joy. You're blushing," Elisha teased.

"I am not." Joy withdrew the smile on her face.

"Well, I'm not going to prod any further. Do your thing, just be careful. You know what I went through."

"I know. And I will. Thanks for looking out for me."

"Always." Elisha smiled at her. "I'll check on you later. Love you, girl."

"Love you too."

"Bye," they said in unison.

Joy looked away from the blank screen and back at the flowers in her kitchen. She checked the time and quickly went to her room to slip into her favorite summer dress. Before showing up on set today, she had to find something nice to wear afterwards for her trip to Carlington Home Furnishings.

Chapter Seven

"WHERE WOULD YOU LIKE me to put these lamps, Mr. Carlington?" Amanda, one of Chase's store associates, carefully held up a unique turquoise ceramic lamp. The distinctive waves down the sides highlighted by silver accents provided the perfect base for the white linen shade. "They came in this morning from one of the suppliers."

Chase examined the lamp and then glanced across the large showroom filled with high-end furniture. "Put it in the window on that new side table. And swap out the handwoven rugs for the hand knotted ones."

"Yes, sir." Amanda nodded and walked away.

Chase headed to the breakroom area separated from a neighboring block of executive offices as his store manager dashed in through the rear exit.

"Hey, Mr. Carlington!" Malcolm waved at Chase as he hurriedly clocked in on the desk computer near the back door. "Thanks again for covering me. I know you were planning on working in the woodshop today." The floor manager spoke of the detached warehouse sharing the modest five-acre lot that was connected by a long, covered breezeway with a metal roof.

"Oh, that's alright. Things happen," Chase calmly spoke of the man's reported flat tire. "I was planning on being here most of the day anyway. Did you get everything squared away?"

"Yes, thank you." The manager huffed as he fought to slow his breathing. "I was towed to the shop right up the street and I walked here."

"You walked here?" Chase questioned with a raised brow. "I would have given you a ride."

"No, it's okay. With that workout I have an excuse to not exercise later." The heavyset man chuckled while securing an insulated lunch pail inside of the oversized stainless-steel refrigerator. The adjoining open kitchen was equipped with a wall of cabinets stocked with paper products, condiments, and jugs of distilled water. "Is it busy today?"

"On and off. We have a few browsing. Jason and Amanda are on the floor and Jenny is at the front desk." Chase looked past him through the slit on the back door which oversaw the lot that held a fleet of trucks. "But we do have quite a few deliveries going out today. When you get settled, be sure to check on the drivers and let me know if you need anything."

"I will." Malcolm smoothed his single-cuff button-up short-sleeve shirt against his body.

"Was the new sales associate coming in today?" Chase asked as he looked at the large TV mounted above a long counter with screens that rotated from the weather, stock market, and other daily broadcast displays.

"No, she's part-time and will be back tomorrow. The assistant manager is coming in for a few hours to shadow me today. I'm going to post the new schedule later today. I gave all the details of the new hires to the HR manager earlier this week."

"Okay, good. Well, I'll leave you to your work." Chase patted his pocket and soon realized that he had left his cell behind the front counter. Just then, the familiar sound of the soft door chime rang through the store, signaling the arrival of a new customer.

Chase emerged from the back office and recognized a familiar face in the showroom. He watched as Joy casually browsed his signature collection just released to market. It was one he hoped would help him expand his business, especially as he contemplated opening a second branch. This winter, he looked forward to showcasing his latest pieces at an event in New York City with hopes to gain global exposure.

"It's a surprise to see you here," Chase said as he walked to where Joy stood.

"Oh, hey." She glanced back at him and squinted as if surprised. "It's Chase, right?"

Chase flashed his million-dollar smile and nodded. "You remembered." He was easily mesmerized by her glowing skin and captivating smile. The ornate jewel-laced barrette clipped the twisted front portion of her dark hair beautifully. It allowed him to see her lightly made-up cheekbones and radiant doe eyes as the loose curls of her locks fell to her shoulders.

Joy allowed the short purse straps at the bend in her elbow to slide down to her hands. "Well, it's hard to forget someone who sent flowers to my house." The motion of her eyes emphasized her point.

Chase offered a bashful grin as he slipped an ink pen in the front pocket of his collared shirt. "So, you got them."

"Yeah, I got them." Joy rested her hand lightly on the back of a sofa. "Thank you."

"You're welcome." He carefully moved closer to her. "I was confused when they sent me an alert that they had to be reissued. Was everything okay with the delivery?"

"Yes, they just forgot the card, so I didn't know who had sent them at first." Joy shrugged as if she was living in that moment. "But I have the card now, and they sent another fresh bouquet as an apology."

"Oh … another bouquet free of charge? That's good service." *I'll have to use them again*, he thought. "I hope the hydrangeas met with your approval."

"Yeah, they did." Joy's mystified stare lingered because hydrangeas, especially the bluish green variation, were her favorite. "Thank you," she said again.

"You're very welcome." Chase studied her carefully, memorizing details about Joy he hadn't noticed before. The faint dimples in her cheeks came and went as she spoke and the small birthmark on her shoulder was unveiled by subtle movements of the thin strap of her sundress. "So, what brings you here?" He took a step closer to her and raised a brow as he asked, "Were you looking for something in particular?"

Joy's lips parted slightly at the way he asked that last question. There was an intense attraction between them that was palpable in the room. The scent of his cologne momentarily entranced her just as her glowing innocence arrested his attention. Joy instinctively turned her head to another part of the room, breaking the trance between them, as she blushed at his words. "Uh, why do you ask? Do you work here?" She looked back at him after quickly composing herself.

"I own it," Chase confidently answered. "That's my name on the sign out there." He pointed to the large structure outside the window just off the highway.

Joy's attention momentarily shifted to the stone engraved sign that bore his name. She met his gaze again and nodded knowingly. "Well, the truth is that I found out you owned this store before coming here."

"Oh, you did?" Chase's grin widened as he folded his arms confidently across his inflated chest. "Is that right?"

"Yes." Joy quietly exhaled. "To be completely transparent, I just wanted to apologize for the way I treated you the other day. I'm sorry."

Chase dared to touch and hold her hand just as he had when they first met. "No need to apologize. You didn't do anything wrong." When another customer entered the showroom, he scaled back his advances by removing his hand from hers. "You didn't know me, and when I thought about the way I must've sounded, I don't blame you. But..." He briefly paused.

"But what?" She curiously leaned closer.

Chase surveyed the furniture gallery, pinpointing the whereabouts of his employees to visually measure whether their distance put them out of earshot. "But if you're here to give me another chance to take you out, I'm willing to ask again if I need to." Moistening his lips, Chase confidently asked, "Will you join me for dinner tonight?"

There it was again, those words she secretly wanted to hear, but publicly shied away from. He checked all of her boxes: Christian, no children, educated, and successful. Although she never asked God that he share her racial background, that was now something Joy seriously considered.

"Look, that's really nice of you, but I just got out of a relationship and—"

Disappointed, Chase finished her sentence, "And you just don't want to get into anything new with someone else right now. Am I right?"

The awkward emotion welling up inside of her betrayed the intention she had when she decided to drive to his store. "Well ... yeah, that's kind of it."

Chase chuckled in response. "I didn't propose. I just asked you to dinner."

"I know..." His words drew a smile from her. "I just think I need some time to sort through my feelings, you know."

Chase masked his disappointment well. He reached into the front pocket of his khaki slacks and pulled out a business card. Joy watched as he scribbled his personal cell phone number on the back.

"After you've sorted through your feelings, give me a call. Maybe I can even get that new headshot done." He winked, slowly handing the business card to her. "I hope I hear from you soon. Thanks for stopping by."

Joy stood motionless as Chase left her standing alone on the showroom floor. He didn't look back, not even once, as he disappeared to the back of the store. She flipped the card between her fingers as she exhaled a deep breath and walked out of the front double doors.

Chapter Eight

CHASE LED HIS HORSE back into the cool refuge of the stable just below the large cluster of southern live oak trees. He glanced at his watch and pursed his lips before removing the horse's saddle. The sun had been up for nearly an hour, two hours since the scheduled time Booker was to meet him on the ranch, but his brother was nowhere to be found.

This is why I don't like dealing with him, he thought.

Booker had promised that he would help with the horses this weekend. Chase figured it would be a way for him to show their father that he could indeed count on Booker while leaving him alone to manage his own affairs. After Chase closed the horse in a stall and turned on the ventilation fans, he phoned his brother. No answer. He kicked a nearby watering can that caused a stir among the horses as it clamored against the floor.

"Is everything all right?" Travis, Leroy's son, rushed in from outside. He looked at the bucket that was rocking back and forth on its side and stared at Chase.

"I'm good, Travis." Chase waved off the disturbance as he calmed his horse.

"How's Impartial?" Travis asked about the horse Chase petted, named Impartially True.

"She's fine. The noise just spooked her, that's all." Chase offered the filly a handful of grain.

"Oh, okay. Well, all the horses have been fed, and two of my friends are helping in the dog kennels." Travis smiled at Chase, revealing his gold-capped teeth. "Did you need me to sponge your horse off? I just got through with your other two."

Chase looked at him and nodded. "Yeah, sponge her off and make sure she gets some water. And let the trainer know that she's back in the stable."

"Okay, I'll do that." Travis turned to retrieve a sponge, but he stopped short and stared back at Chase.

"What is it?" Chase met his gaze.

"I was watching you out there. You can still handle her like a pro." Travis walked back in his direction. "Why'd you ever stop jockeying?"

Chase's response lingered with hesitation. He didn't like talking about why he quit such a rewarding sport that he was so good at. Especially at a time when he had jockeyed a horse that reached the pinnacle of performance at the Preakness Stakes, a horse race second in the competition series preceded by the Kentucky Derby and followed by the Belmont Stakes. The combination of these three competitions made up the famed Triple Crown races.

"Besides the fact that I hit my growth spurt?" He successfully drew laughter from Travis, noting that jockeys are normally shorter than five-feet-six inches and kept at a much lighter weight than his now muscular five-foot-ten-inch frame. "Even if that hadn't happened, let's just say that it was time to move on." As Chase released the harness strap that cradled his chin and pulled his helmet off, he recalled how his father soured his name by convincing a trainer to later inject the horse with a banned substance he had ridden to Preakness victory at the age of only sixteen years old. The substance was found when Chase attempted a follow-up victory at the Belmont Stakes.

"I see." Travis nodded, understanding by the look on Chase's face that he should just leave the topic alone. "Well, if you need me for anything else, I'll be over there after I water your horse." He pointed toward the barn that held bales of hay and pallets of grain.

"Okay." Chase nodded at him. "And thanks for showing up on such short notice. You were a great help this morning."

Travis offered a humbled smile. "You got it, man. Any time. Be sure to tell your dad we said thank you for the job."

Chase watched as Travis led Impartially True to a watering trough and then to an area just outside the stable. He tossed the helmet in his hands in a repetitive circular motion in front of him a few times before securing it between his arm and the side of his body. If his father knew the day rate promised to Travis and his friend, he'd have a fit.

In the muggy heat of their terrain, Chase couldn't morally justify Phil's proposed amount to those men for how hard they worked in those conditions. Especially since his father had willingly agreed to pay a significantly larger amount to their white counterparts hired on as new full-time employees *with* benefits. Since the work experience was the same as well as the conditions, Chase figured why not also their pay.

After showering in the nearby station specifically installed for the trainers, Chase swapped out his riding boots and helmet for comfortable walking shoes and a sporty baseball cap. He stored his other gear away to be laundered and walked out of the changing area. He reached for his ringing cell and stared at the incoming call from a concealed number, evident by the words, *Anonymous Caller*, displayed on the screen. By the time he decided to answer, the ringing had stopped. When Chase looked up again, he met eyes with his brother.

"Where have you been?" Chase questioned Booker. "You were supposed to be here over two hours ago."

"You don't own me." Booker glared at his brother who could almost pass for his twin. "If you must know, I overslept, all right. It's not like I tried to be late." He held the side of his head as he closed his reddened eyes, frowning from the stench of the animals. "I need some fresh air." Booker walked back outside to a bench underneath one of the trees.

Chase closely followed Booker to the bench where he now sat. "This is my last time covering for you. I had to get Travis and his friends to help because you're always missing in action.

Dad is still holding me responsible for things *you're* supposed to do." He angrily pointed at him.

"Dad isn't interested in what I should be doing around here." Booker sat up to defend himself. "As far as he's concerned, I've gotten my inheritance and all he wants is a return on his investment by getting work out of me."

"Booker, do you hear yourself? When are you going to get it together? They don't owe you anything. You had Mom paying your bills behind Dad's back. And when he found out, that was cut short. You're thirty-two, practically homeless, and—"

"Hey, I'm not homeless!" Booker shouted at him, and then immediately held the crown of his head again as he winced.

"Well, what would you call it?" Chase glared at him. "Dad won't let you in the house, and the closest you get to sleeping on the property is in their RV that Mom begged him to let you live in. He won't even pay for a place for you to live anymore."

"You're always going to see me for who I was, aren't you? No matter how hard I try to redeem myself, you just see the old me." Booker scratched the side of his gruffy beard and grunted.

"The old you is the you right now, Booker. Stop *trying* to redeem yourself and just do it!" Chase's loud voice startled a flock of birds from the extended tree branches above them. "It's always somebody else's fault with you. When silver came up missing from Mom's China closet, you didn't know how that happened, even though you were the only one around that day. And you said nothing when Dad started looking at Ms. Dinah sideways. And when his handmade silk ties from Italy mysteriously disappeared, you didn't understand how, but you were the only other one who had access to his *private* closet at the office downtown. And now I hear that someone's been using his credit card, but I don't have to guess about that either, do I?"

Booker's eyes sobered with surprise. "He knows about that?"

"What do you think?" Chase glared at him with disgust. "Do you want to go to jail because of this?"

"No," Booker groaned and turned away from Chase, "of course not." He needlessly adjusted the tattered old jeans he wore.

The constant accusations hurled Booker's way only drove him to a darker place of shame. After he dropped out of college during his first semester, Phil had threatened to similarly drop him from his will. It wasn't long after Booker had defied his father that he saw doors of opportunities close around him. With others in their circle, Phil was that powerful. He often heard his father spitting a southern aphorism, *I'm the tallest hog at the trough*, if someone tried to cross him. In response, Booker would grumble behind his back, *The tallest hog is usually the first to be slaughtered*.

"You've got to stop this."

"Chase, Dad's not going to send me to jail or anywhere else for that matter. He may call himself punishing me by pulling that RV act, but he would only go so far with it," Booker grumbled.

Chase curiously stared at him, recognizing that the relationship between them and their father, though different in nature, was clearly a tolerated one.

"You're smashed." Chase propped one of his feet on the bench beside his brother with an elbow just above his knee. "You don't look like you're in any shape to help out today."

"I'm not smashed, I'm tired. There's a difference. I was up late last night." Booker slumped on the seat and rested his head against the back of the bench with closed eyes. "All I have to do is tell those other guys what to do. That's not that hard."

"But you have to be awake to do that." Chase stomped his foot on the bench. "Get up!"

"I'm awake!" Booker snapped, grimacing in annoyance. "Do you know what it feels like to be up half the night working?" Booker had resorted to earning quick money by working at a friend's nightclub a couple weekends out of the month.

"Yes, I do." Chase matched his combative glare. "I have my own business, remember?"

"Oh, here we go. Are you going to rub that in my face again?" Booker scoffed.

"What are you talking about?" Chase questioned, squinting at his brother.

"The fact that you finished school, got your degrees, certifications, licenses, *and* Dad's blessings." Booker named them all by counting on his fingers one by one.

"I'm not rubbing anything in your face. I worked for everything that I have. We both got money from Grandpa. I started a business and bought a house with mine. What did you do with yours?"

Booker rolled his eyes.

"And what Dad gives me, I wouldn't call it a blessing," Chase continued. "If so, I would be in my woodshop right now and not out here doing *your* job."

Booker abruptly stood on his feet. "Well, I'm here now. I guess you can get back to your perfect life." He walked past Chase and toward the stables but turned back once and said in a condescending tone, "And do me a favor, if it's not too much for you."

"What's that?" Chase stared at him.

"Be sure to tell Dad that I showed up." Booker straightened the white T-shirt across his body which bore the bold-printed words: Carlington Ranch. "I don't feel like an interrogation today."

Chase stared at his brother, who didn't bother waiting for an answer as he disappeared inside the stable. He quickly texted his father, letting him know about Booker, and immediately left the property.

Chapter Nine

Joy scrolled through her phone for the third time over the past five minutes. No new calls. No new messages. She grabbed Chase's business card from her dresser and checked it against the numbers already saved in her cell. After Joy saw that she had indeed saved Chase's information correctly, she sighed to herself.

"Hey, did you still want to catch lunch and go to that art gallery today?" Tiana slowly questioned after she poked her head into Joy's bedroom.

"The opening *you* said you wanted to go to? Uh, yeah, I was planning on it. Why?" Joy slid Chase's card underneath a box of facial tissue on her desk and turned away from the vanity mirror where she sat. "Don't tell me you're backing out when you were the one who convinced me to ditch the festival because it's your birthday. Not to mention the artist you wanted to check out who's premiering his work."

"I was called into work today," Tiana groaned. "They're short-staffed and I'm really hoping to get promoted soon."

She entered the room and hugged Joy around the shoulders. "I'm sorry I had you cancel going to the cultural park festival. Raincheck?"

"I guess." Joy shrugged and patted Tiana's arms wrapped around her.

"Believe me, my other friends aren't thrilled about my canceling on them either. Do y'all really think I want to work on my birthday?" Tiana stood upright and placed a hand on her hip.

Joy smirked and playfully rolled her eyes away.

"Hey, if it's not too late, I may get off in time where we can still check out the festival. You know how things usually get started a little slow at these things anyway."

"Nah, that's all right. When it gets too late, you know how the crowd changes."

"Yeah, you're right." Tiana made a face as she carefully adjusted the tight backs of the brand-new earrings she received as a birthday gift from a close relative.

"Besides, I'm a little tired anyway. Between working on set and getting things ready for classes next week, I'm worn out. I'll probably just grab something to eat after meeting with Professor Sommers and go to bed early."

"You sound like an old lady, you know." Tiana giggled as she walked back toward the door.

Joy smiled at her. "That wouldn't be the first time I've heard that. But whatever."

"Just promise me that you won't be working ... *on anything*," Tiana emphasized as she stood in the doorway with a hand on the knob. "You have been wearing yourself out this past week. Take a minute for yourself and unwind. I promise you, one night off isn't going to make you fall behind."

"I will, *mother*," Joy teased. "I'll catch up with you in the morning."

"Bye, girl." Tiana waved at her and moments later Joy heard the front door near the living room slam shut.

Joy blew a light breath of air from her pouted lips that gently disturbed the strands of her bangs. As she looked in the mirror, she smoothed the sides of her ponytail and grabbed a sheet of tissue from its holder to remedy the over-age of lip gloss from the corners of her mouth. Chase's card slid from beneath the container after she had accidentally dragged it across the desk. Joy picked up the card and placed it in the top drawer of her vanity.

It was embarrassing to admit, even to herself, that she had called this man earlier from a blocked number. But when she listened to his message greeting, Joy was once again drawn to what could be. The silkiness of his voice washed over her, and unexpectedly she was curious to find out more about him. The way he nonchalantly handed over his personal cell phone number in the furniture store, making it clear of his intentions, was smooth. Chase was careful not to badger her and confident enough to walk away. His self-assurance was refreshing, and Joy wanted to know more about him.

"Hello," Joy answered her cell, startled from her thoughts.

"Hey, are you busy?" Michelle asked. "I know I was supposed to call earlier, but Justin came over *unexpectedly*."

"Didn't you tell him to stop doing that?"

"Yes, I did, but I didn't feel like arguing today. I just wanted to let him see his child so he could go on his way." Michelle sighed. "But Clayton did seem happy about him being here, so I let it go."

"Oh, well, that's good," Joy said slowly.

"What's going on with you? Are you sure that you're not busy?" Michelle's tone held reservation. "I can tell when you're not paying attention. What's up?"

"Girl, it's nothing. I'm just tired. I have a lot on my plate and—"

"And you're thinking about Chase again, aren't you?"

An emerging smile crept across Joy's face. She tried to stifle it because her best friend would still be able to hear it in her voice if she didn't. "What are you talking about? I've only seen the guy twice."

"Yeah, but I've never heard you talk about anyone that you've dated as much as you have about him."

"But we're not dating," Joy reminded her.

"Exactly," Michelle added.

Joy pressed her lips together as she grabbed a stack of photos she had printed from her first day on the movie set. She sifted through them and separated the ones of Chase.

"What do you think I should do? He seems really nice, and I think I'm attracted to him."

"You think? Oh, Joy, you know that you are. Stop fighting it and just go out with him already."

"Well, he hasn't tried to call me or anything."

"So, you haven't seen him since that day at his store?" Michelle questioned.

"No, nothing." Joy propped her elbow on the desk, pushing his pictures away in the process. "Not even on the movie set which wraps soon. I thought for sure he would've emailed me or something."

"Joy, how can the man contact you when you haven't given him any of your information?"

"Well, I found out about him and even went to his store." Joy crossed her legs and tugged at the white frayed shorts she wore. "He knows where I live, and his sister has all my other information."

"Really, Joy, do you hear yourself? His *sister* has your information. Did you just say that? If he showed up at your place unannounced after you've already turned him down, how would that look?"

Joy refrained from responding as she twisted her lips to one side and rolled her eyes.

"He's made it clear that he's into you," Michelle continued. "I don't think he's into games. Didn't you say that he's like forty or something?"

"Now you know I didn't say that!" Joy burst into laughter. "He's only twenty-nine. And I don't think that's too old. I mean, look at the guys we've gone out with. They're so imma-ture. Do you think he's too old?"

"Girl, I'm just playing with you." Michelle chuckled. "No, twenty-nine *is* pushing it, but I don't think it's *too* old. My point is that he's probably the serious settle down type. From what you've told me, he's doing the thing *and* he's saved." Michelle noted how Joy had bragged about all the qualities Chase pos-sessed, outlining the impressive things he had accomplished before the age of thirty. "Just because he's not who you'd usually date doesn't mean that he's not worth your time. It's okay for you to call him. If you don't, I'm sure the next girl will."

"I guess you're right." Joy fidgeted with her manicured French-tip fingernails. She hadn't considered that possibility. Chase could very well lose interest in her if she didn't express the mutual feelings they shared.

"So, you're gonna call him?" Michelle asked, seeking confir-mation.

"Yes, I'm going to call." Joy exhaled, challenged by the thought that Chase would view her as the pursuer.

"When?"

"When I come back from meeting Professor Sommers."

"Professor Sommers? On a Saturday?" Michelle curiously questioned.

"Yeah. Do you remember her?"

"I don't think so."

Joy explained that Professor Sommers, now more of a mentor to her, had left around the same time Michelle had at the end of their freshman year. After returning this summer, she resumed her position at the university and became the owner of a new photography studio that was set to open soon.

"Oh, okay. And you want to get a paid internship or something." Michelle filled in the blanks.

"Something like that."

"Well, call me tomorrow after church. I want to hear all about Mr. Chase Carlington."

"That's *if* I talk to him. If he doesn't answer the phone, I'm not calling back," Joy said with a bit of an attitude.

"Just leave a message if he doesn't answer." Michelle couldn't help but chuckle at Joy's hint of arrogance, finding it both impulsive and amusing. "He has a life just like you do," she reminded her.

"I know. I just don't want him to think I'm trying to be all up on him like that."

"Joy, I know you. You already are." Michelle giggled. "You wouldn't still be talking about him if you weren't."

Joy turned the prints of Chase face down on her desk and walked toward her bedroom window. "Bye, Michelle."

"Why do you have to be like that? You know I'm telling the truth." Michelle laughed harder.

"Whatever, I've got to get ready before I'm late."

"Okay, I'll let you go." Her laughter subsided. "But seriously, don't play too hard to get, you may end up missing out."

Joy pondered Michelle's advice after their call ended. She was right, in more ways than one. Michelle was there when she secretly dated a guy that was indeed way too old for her, one that was way too immature, and another that was way too clingy. And then the latest one who ran serious game on her and brought drugs into her home. At times, Michelle knew Joy better than she knew herself. And the fact that she was spot on about Chase unnerved her. She hadn't acted this way about a guy since her first crush in middle school. Giddy about the possibility and eager to learn everything about him.

She had decided that after her appointment with Professor Sommers, she was going to call him and see where things could go—if anywhere.

Chapter Ten

THE QUAINT COFFEE SHOP on the corner of Main Street and College Crossing was just ending its lunch rush. The bistro, Ashton's, known for its famous cheesecake streusel muffin with white chocolate chips and popular cream cheese topped cinnamon sticky bun, was a city favorite among residents and visitors alike. Joy had enjoyed many early morning pit stops there on her way to class over the years. It had become a regular staple every Thursday since their doors opened in the heart of town.

"Hey, Joy, over here!" Professor Sommers called from a circular wooden table on the far-left side of the room.

Joy snapped her head in the direction of her voice and smiled as their eyes met. She raised a hand in acknowledgement and walked toward the table her beloved mentor had held for the two of them.

"Hi, Professor Sommers, I'm so glad to see you." Joy excitedly hugged the slim woman in her late thirties, average height with blonde hair before taking a seat across the table from her.

"Likewise, Joy. But before we go any further, enough with the formalities. I'm no longer your professor. Come spring, you'll be more of a colleague. Please, just call me Wynter."

"Oh, okay ... *Wynter*." Joy secured her purse on the hook of the chair back. "I was surprised to see your name a couple weeks ago as I was registering for a last-minute class I wanted to add. When I noticed you were back, I just had to email you."

"I'm so glad you contacted me." Wynter scooted her chair closer to the table. "Sorry it took so long to get back with you, but it's been a whirlwind getting settled here again." She glanced at her cell phone and typed a quick text before looking back at Joy. "And I'm still incredibly busy."

"I can imagine. Moving can take a lot out of a person. Are you here to stay?" Joy asked just as a waiter placed a clear cup of peach iced tea and the famed cheesecake streusel muffin on a small ceramic dish in front of her. "I didn't order this," she said to the gentleman.

"Oh, I ordered your favorite muffin. I know how you like the white chocolate chips in it." Wynter glanced at the waiter and then looked back at Joy. "At least I hope it's still your favorite."

"You remembered." Joy looked up from the saucer and nodded. "Yes, it's still my favorite. I actually still stop in at least once a week for this muffin." It was an indulgent pleasure they had in common. Ever since Joy nervously sat with her that second week of classes freshman year, being that Wynter Sommers was a professor and she a wide-eyed teenager, they gradually formed an acquaintanceship as regulars in the café.

"It's still my favorite too." Wynter smiled at the waiter as he rested a saucer in front of her as well. Her attention quickly returned to her phone as it chimed with a new message. "Please excuse me, I'm breaking in a new babysitter." Wynter typed another text and sighed as she placed the phone on the table beside the white ceramic saucer. When she looked up, she noticed Joy silently praying over her small meal, her hands clasped together in a gesture of reverence. Wynter took this opportunity to whisper a prayer of thanksgiving too.

"So, how does it feel to be this close to graduation?" Wynter took a bite of her muffin.

At first, Joy quietly sipped from her cup, and then moaned in satisfaction. "It feels really good and a little scary all at the same time. If you know what I mean?"

"I do, and its normal." Wynter nodded with understanding. "I've heard so many students in your shoes say the same thing. But with your grades and work ethic, you have nothing to be concerned about. Just keep doing what you're doing. You won't have to look for opportunities, opportunities will follow you."

"Thank you for the encouragement. And that's something I wanted to talk to you about. An opportunity to work in an actual studio with an established photographer."

Wynter rested her back against the chair and grinned. "From what I hear, you're doing very well on your own."

Joy blushed at the attention she had been getting around town from past clients.

"Well, I learned from the best," she complimented Wynter. "I couldn't have done it without you."

Wynter gently smiled as she swiped her wavy blonde hair behind her ears and adjusted the gold-trimmed glasses over her blue eyes.

"I'll never forget how much time you took out of your schedule to mentor me when you barely knew me." Joy peeled the paper ridges away from the muffin and took a small bite. She brushed crumbs from her fingertips and cleared a few pieces from her lips as well with a napkin.

"When I see something special in my students, I can't help but nurture that gift in any way that I can. You're a natural and it actually made my job easy."

"I was all over the place my first semester, but when I changed my minor and had you as a professor the next semester, I couldn't thank God enough." Joy instinctively reached for the small cross dangling from the silver necklace she wore.

"Well, I'm glad to have been some help to you." Wynter lowered her eyes onto her saucer and picked at the white chocolate chip chunks with her freshly manicured nails.

"I hated to see you go." The radiant glow on Joy's face mirrored the gratefulness in her heart.

"I hated to leave, but it's all come full circle." Wynter sipped sparingly from her cup. "And with the occasional emails back and forth, I'm glad we never lost touch."

"Yeah, me too." Joy's attention momentarily shifted to a passerby who walked to the counter behind where they were seated. She didn't see the man's face, but she would recognize that lean muscular build anywhere. Days of studying his frame in the photos she took prompted her to memorize things about him an ordinary person may not notice at first glance, like the small scar just above his elbow on the back of his left arm.

"Do you know him?" Wynter followed Joy's fixed gaze on Chase.

Joy looked away from Chase, who was placing an order at the front counter, and back to Wynter. "Sort of ..." The expression on her face was telling.

"I see." Wynter smiled as she checked her phone again. She then scribbled a note on a small flip pad from her purse and tore the sheet along its perforated edge. "It's my babysitter again. I'm sorry, but I have to go. Here's my new number and the address to the studio."

Joy took the small piece of paper Wynter handed to her.

"I left my new business cards at home as I was rushing over here. Long story." Wynter folded her muffin in a napkin and adjusted the designer purse onto her shoulder as she stood. "Give me a couple weeks to get things sorted out with the space and I'll have you come in. How does that sound?"

"That sounds great, thanks." Joy nodded, excited about the opportunities of working with her on a professional level. "It was so good seeing you. I can walk out with you," she offered as she hugged her mentor again.

"Oh, no, stay and finish your muffin. Besides, I think you *sort of* want to spend a little time with him." Wynter glanced at Chase, who was now retrieving his order, and winked as she picked up her drink. "See you later," she said with a wave and walked out of the café.

Joy sat back down as she avoided eye contact with Chase. It was silly of her to pretend that she didn't see him, but that was exactly what she was doing. She exhaled a deep breath as he walked past her to an unoccupied table a few feet away. Joy watched as he sat down with his back to her.

Maybe he really didn't see me, she reasoned. Joy reached for her cell and pulled up his number.

Hi, it's Joy, she texted. *You gave me this number at your store.*

After sending the simple message, Joy waited to see if he would respond. She watched as he pulled his phone from a side pocket, but just as quickly pushed it back inside the open flap of his cargo shorts. Chase squirted sanitizer into the palm of his hands and vigorously rubbed them together. He lowered his head for a moment, and then proceeded to devour a stacked turkey and cheese sandwich as if it were his last.

Joy sent another message. *This is my number. Call when you get a chance.*

This time, Chase didn't even look at the phone. He finished his sandwich and drank every ounce of his strawberry lemonade. Joy stared at him as he pushed his chair back and walked to the garbage can positioned near the tall double glass doors. He tossed the empty plate and cup in the trash and walked out of the restaurant.

Joy sat dumbfounded, a little embarrassed even. She quietly finished her muffin and remotely started her vehicle before exiting the building. Maybe the scenarios she had played in her mind about the two of them were just mind games. She could admit that she was a little naïve when it came to men, but not completely oblivious to the games they could run. But never in a million years did she ever think that a white man would have her pining after him.

As she approached her vehicle, Joy looked down at the incoming call displayed on her phone. It was Chase.

"Hello?" she asked, her voice laced with hesitation.

"Hey, it's Chase. I just got your text. Can you talk?" he asked.

Joy switched the call to speaker mode and then opened her car door. She scanned the parking lot but didn't see him anywhere.

"Hello, are you there?" Chase questioned, with his voice now holding a similar reservation.

"I'm here," Joy answered as she sat inside her vehicle. "And yes, I can talk."

"Good. I'm glad you finally contacted me." Chase chuckled to himself. "You've been on my mind."

"I have?" Joy genuinely sounded surprised. "I haven't seen you on set lately."

"Were you looking for me?" Chase flirted.

Joy squeezed her eyes shut, wanting to take back her last statement. *He might think I'm more interested in him than he is in me.*

Once again, Chase asked, "Are you there?"

"Yes, I'm here," Joy repeated, reworking her thoughts as to not sound so interested.

"I just figured that since the film wraps soon, you'd be there to see how things are going, being an investor and all."

"Oh, how did you know I was an investor?" Chase asked with curiosity, sounding as if he was smiling as he spoke.

Once again, Joy cringed in embarrassment from her outburst. By expressing how much she knew about him, Joy inadvertently revealed how into him she really was. She had already stopped by his store, admitted to looking him up online, and was now tracking him like a backstage groupie.

"It was posted somewhere," Joy flatly answered, hoping to mask her attraction, and then changed the subject. "So, tell me a little about yourself."

Chase cleared his throat, and then he hummed as if in contemplation. "*Hmmm* ... well, you already know that I own a furniture store."

"Yes ... and the furnishings are very nice by the way." Joy scrolled through her phone and pulled up his website again.

"Thanks," Chase said with appreciation. "Besides designing my own custom pieces, I enjoy riding horses and I'm not a bad golfer on occasions." He chuckled.

"Oh, a golfer." Joy giggled as she thought about her father and the recent hobby he had taken up. Before she realized it, "my dad would love you," slipped out of her mouth.

Her family barely knew anything about the last guy she dated and mentioning Chase to them was nowhere on the radar, not even a little bit. But there was something about him that caused her to speak without even thinking.

"Oh, your dad is a golfer?" Chase sounded genuinely interested to know more.

"I would say so. I mean, he's only been doing it for the past couple of years but has gotten pretty good at it lately. He's even trying to train my little nephew." Joy chuckled.

"It can be an addictive sport, but I haven't been on the green in a while. Work pretty much keeps me busy."

"I'm sure." Joy tapped her fingers on the gear shift, watching as people entered and left the café.

"So, I hear this is your senior year at the university. Do you plan on staying in Simpson?"

Joy assumed it had to be Patricia again who had filled Chase in on her background. She figured there wasn't much he didn't know about her. If he had scoured her website like she had done his, he was sure to know that she was a Christian, too.

"Uh, I don't know yet. I'm weighing my options, trying to field some opportunities. God will make it plain soon enough."

"That He will," Chase agreed. "Do you believe that He directs our paths?"

"One hundred percent. I just think many of us may not listen to His direction. So, that's what my prayer is right now, to hear His voice and follow where He leads."

"Me too." Chase's tone softened. "I'm learning how to not only listen, Joy, but to also obey."

"Yes, Chase, me too." She became excited at their faith connection. "I was just reading during my study this morning about submitting my works to the Lord. It was so clear to me."

"Are you kidding me? I just read that very same Scripture this morning too!" Chase's enthusiasm echoed the excitement bubbling inside Joy.

"*Commit your works to the Lord and your thoughts will be established,*" they spontaneously recited Proverbs 16:3 in unison. Soon after, they both burst into laughter.

"Wow, that's amazing," Joy said, easily lowering her guard. "What church do you go to?"

Effortlessly the two spoke about their growing trust in God, each professing their faith in Jesus Christ as Lord and Savior. Something Joy hadn't been able to do as openly with any other man she had dated until now. Often, when the subject of God arose in a conversation referring to salvation and having a personal relationship with Jesus Christ, it was regularly met with a stance of, *I grew up in the church, my father's a pastor,* or *I talk to God every day.* None of those responses clearly answered the question she had specifically asked.

As the conversation continued, the bond she was beginning to form with Chase was reminiscent of the heart song she had played for God. Nobody else knew exactly what she wanted as well as Him, and the longer she spoke with Chase, the more she envisioned a real possibility with him. Aside from the physical attraction, Joy anticipated learning more about his spiritual walk with God. Considering how Patricia explained their upbringing, she was naturally a little hesitant. But the longer she conversed with Chase, the more those hesitations drifted away.

"It was great talking to you, Joy. I don't want to hang up," he softly chuckled, "but I'm at my store now. If you're not busy, would you like to get together later? I'd really like to see you."

Joy looked back at Ashton's and smiled, realizing that Chase was oblivious that she was ever there. "Later? Okay ... where?"

"The LaGrange Hotel. I can pick you up for dinner, say around six-thirty?"

Joy was familiar with the upscale restaurant attached to the five-star hotel. She remembered staying at the hotel in the past when Zachary graduated college, and more recently for a friend's graduation banquet. The fine dining establishment offered the best cuisine in the city, and Joy was impressed that Chase wanted their first date to be there.

"The attire is semi-formal. Is that okay with you?" he conferred with her for approval.

"Sure," Joy beamed with excitement, but successfully curbed her enthusiasm. "That's fine."

"Great." Chase sounded as if he was smiling behind his words too. "I'll call you when I'm on my way."

"Okay," Joy answered just as a message popped up from Tiana. "See you in a few hours," she told him before ending the call.

Two o'clock. She had just enough time to catch a nap and revitalize her tired eyes. But after reading Tiana's text, Joy realized that time would be better served investigating the messages Rico had sent through her friend. Leave it up to him to find a workaround to all the roadblocks she had put in place.

Although busy at work, the screenshot texts Tiana forwarded from him to Joy spoke volumes. It was bad enough that he had dragged her friend into this crazy mess, but to profess that it was all in the name of love made Joy livid. She wasn't sure if she should take him at face value or read deeper behind his text to her:

I gave it all up for you and want to make things right. I love you. Please forgive me. See you soon.

Joy pulled up Tiana's number but decided against calling her. Since she was being considered for a promotion, Joy refrained from contacting her friend at work for more details. However, she needed to know if he had sent her anything else. Joy just wanted to be rid of the past and have a fresh start apart from the drama.

Now with Chase scheduled to pick her up from home, Joy had to contend with whether Rico was back in town and if he would dare to come to her home. Frustrated, she sent Tiana an apology text, put her car in gear, and quickly drove home.

Chapter Eleven

JOY SNATCHED THE EYE mask from her face and grunted. The anticipation of dinner at LaGrange with Chase was dampened by Rico's troublesome text. Joy stared at the clock on her wall which read five-nineteen and sat up in bed. Even after a relaxing shower when she arrived home earlier, Joy became restless as she struggled to take a nap. She rolled over in bed and tried to call Rico before going to sleep, but each of her three attempts went straight to voicemail.

It was even more troublesome for Joy when Tiana phoned during her lunch break to inform her that Rico had left her a voicemail too. It confirmed what she had dreaded. Rico had hopped a flight from California to Alabama enroute to see her. Even though she had removed his name from the list of guests allowed through the security gate of the community where she lived, Joy was concerned that a guard who knew Rico as a regular visitor may inadvertently allow him through without checking the log.

In the middle of gargling after brushing her teeth, Joy heard her cell phone ringing in the bedroom. She hurriedly spat in the sink and rushed to her nightstand where she disappointedly groaned. In roughly an hour Chase would be at her door, and she still had to do her makeup and slip into her attire for the evening.

"Hey, Mom." Joy pulled a few sheets of facial tissue from a box on her nightstand and cleared the excess mouthwash from her lips. Although pressed for time to get dressed before she left home, Joy reasoned that if she had allowed the call to go to voicemail, her mother would only phone again, maybe repeatedly, while she was out on her date.

"Hi, Joy. Did you get the package I sent you earlier in the week? I didn't hear anything from you."

"Oh yeah, I got it." Joy divided her attention between her mother and the stunning salmon colored dress sprawled across her king-size bed.

"Well, you could have called and let me know," Margaret said, her voice tinged with irritation.

"I'm sorry, Ma," Joy apologized. "I was just so—"

"Busy, I know." Margaret released a telling chuckle. "If it's not you, it's Josh or Zach. Don't tell me that my baby isn't my baby anymore."

Joy smiled as she sat at her vanity desk and placed her mother on the speaker. "Only if you're planning on having more children," she casually joked, tightening the mini bath robe around her body.

"Now you stop that, this shop is closed," Margaret quipped.

The two shared a pleasant laugh.

"Anyway, how's everything going since classes started? We don't hear much from you nowadays."

"Mom, I'll be there for Labor Day in a couple weeks." Joy chuckled to herself as she applied a thin layer of foundation to her skin, pushing the bonnet on her head back to ensure full coverage.

"And we probably won't see you then. Between you, Michelle, and your other friends, your father and I usually only get to sit down with you for Sunday dinner after church. And then you're on the road back to Simpson."

"But Ma, after Labor Day I'll be there again for fall break." Joy stared at the phone as if Margaret could see her. "For at least three days." She then began applying matte powder to her face with a makeup sponge to set her foundation.

"Do you plan on spending any of it with us?" Margaret questioned.

"Of course I do." With a smile, Joy delicately swept a stroke of blush onto her cheeks using her rose-colored palette. "I promise that I'll spend more time with you guys while I'm there next time."

"Okay, so, you will be at Elisha's housewarming, right?" The sound of her voice was filled with hope as she sought to confirm her daughter's visit for fall break.

"I will, Ma," Joy tenderly replied. Once her mother saw the surprise anniversary party, she was certain she would understand how much both she and Gerald were valued.

"Okay, I'll let your dad know."

"Is he at home?" Joy asked as she glanced at the clock again, noticing that ten minutes had elapsed since she got on the phone with her mother.

"No, he went out to grab dinner for us. We had Jaxon earlier, but Tyler picked him up about an hour ago."

"Oh, okay. How's everybody else doing?" Joy asked, cleansing her fingers from the overage of makeup with a wet wipe from her vanity drawer. She soon abandoned the blush brush for a mascara one and fluffed her full lashes.

Joy vaguely listened as Margaret briefly chatted about her recent volunteer work with Gerald, and the plans she had with him later in the evening. After their call ended, Joy slipped into her dress and sprayed a mist of perfume across the front of her body. She finger-combed the long strands of her hair, trading the ponytail she wore earlier for a style that allowed her tresses to fall past her shoulders. She then attached the back of her diamond stud earrings, gifted to her from Gerald on her eighteenth birthday, and slipped on her embellished ankle-strap evening sandals. Just as she grabbed her matching handbag from the bed and turned the lights out in her room, the home phone rang.

"Yes?" Joy answered, wondering if the call from the security gate was because Chase had arrived much earlier than expected, or because Rico had decided to make a surprise appearance.

"Ms. Maxwell, there's a visitor here to see you, but I do not see his name on the list," the security guard explained. "Did you want me to allow him through?"

Joy's heart began racing as she checked the time again. Chase specifically said six-thirty and it was only five-fifty-seven. When she checked online after talking to Tiana, the two flights arriving from California today both arrived around five-forty-five. She was hoping to be away from her place and at the restaurant before Rico dared to venture her way.

"Who is it?" Joy frowned as she looked out the window, hoping that the plane hadn't caught a tailwind and blew him into town sooner than expected. Where her home was situated, she had a clear path to the security gate, but today a delivery van obstructed her view.

"His ID reads Chase Carlington," the security guard relayed to her.

"Yes, let him through." Joy quickly released the curtains gathered in her hand, allowing them to fall to their normal arrangement. "And please, if Rico Sanders shows up, do not let him in."

"Yes, ma'am. I see that name already noted in the computer."

"Okay thanks, Sam."

That was one thing she was going to have to get used to. Not only was Chase on time, but he was early. Very early. Joy expected that he may have shown up a few minutes before time, but not by thirty minutes. She glanced around her front living room, ensuring that everything was tidy. The pillows on the sofa were fluffed, the rugs lint-free, the stacks of mail were in her office out of view, and the scent from the three-wick candles burned earlier still lingered in the air.

Joy flinched from the ringing doorbell. She had grown used to Rico blowing his horn when he arrived outside that it startled her to hear the chime sound. Although he had opened doors for her and showered her with gifts in the beginning, she now realized it was all just an act. Joy took a deep breath, hoping that Chase would bring a much-needed change. As she peered through the peephole, she sensed he already was.

"Hi, come in." Joy held the door open for Chase as he handed her a large bouquet of red roses.

"Oh, thank you," she said, taking the intricately designed crystal vase from his hands. "They're beautiful."

"Not half as stunning as you are," Chase complimented her as she closed the door behind him. "That dress is gorgeous on you."

"Thank you." Joy placed the vase on the sofa table and turned back to him. "You're looking pretty dapper yourself."

Their laughter filled the air. Chase opened his arms, playfully showing off his crisp lightweight shirt and breathable slacks that perfectly complemented Joy's flowy one-strap shoulder, knee-length dress.

"You have a nice place here." Chase's eyes drifted across the room with delight, landing on several pieces of furniture he had personally designed. "You also have great taste."

"The feeling is mutual." Joy softly smiled in response and nodded knowingly. "Um, would you like something to drink or anything?"

Chase shook his head as he gazed into her eyes. "No, nothing to drink, but I wouldn't mind a hug."

Without hesitation, Joy opened her arms, and he embraced her with a gentle squeeze. The scent of his cologne, the one she had remembered him wearing at his store, hypnotized her. It mingled perfectly with the fragrance of his freshly washed skin. His scent was a tantalizing blend of essential oils suggestive of a cool ocean breeze. As she rested her head against his chest, Joy closed her eyes as Chase gently held her in his arms. Soon their heartbeats fell in sync.

Just then, Chase's phone vibrated in his pocket. Joy looked down and shied away from him.

"I'm sorry." He thumbed across the screen and powered down his cell. "No more interruptions tonight. It's all about you."

Joy gazed at Chase as he held the door open for her. After setting the home alarm, she slipped her wrist through the strap of her clutch purse and followed him outside. Once inside his four-seater convertible Ferrari, Joy whispered to herself, *Thank you, Lord.*

Chapter Twelve

THE SOPHISTICATED AMBIANCE MET with Joy's approval, even more now than in the past. Maybe it was the new crystal chandeliers that cast a shimmery light in the main dining area, or it could have been the unique artwork carefully designed into the reflective gold tiled walls she hadn't noticed before, or maybe it was simply the chivalrous company she kept.

"I didn't know you were going to reserve a private room here." Joy marveled at the effort he had put into their first date. "How did you pull this off on a Saturday night?" In awe, she watched as he pulled a chair from the white linen draped table for her.

Chase slightly adjusted his slacks as he took a seat across from her. "Let's just say I have friends with favors."

"Okay." Joy grinned at his confidence as she accepted a menu from the waiter who asked for their drink orders.

While savoring the four-course meal, Joy discovered they had more in common, including sports, amusement parks, and cultural arts, stemming from their shared passion for history. Chase shared with her his fondness for horseback riding and the filly he was having trained to hopefully enter the Kentucky Derby come spring, and she revealed her affinity for canoeing, picked up from her summer camp days on Lake Lewiston back home. While also being quite a swimmer, Joy clued him in on her skills of water skiing and kayaking as well.

"You are so interesting." Chase reached across the table for Joy's hands after the waiter cleared their dinner plates. "I've never met anyone like you."

Joy rested her petite palms in his. "I feel the same way." She smiled as he carefully caressed her fingers with gentle strokes of his thumbs. "You're so easy to talk to."

"You make it easy." His eyes drifted from hers to the dessert menu placed before them. "Are you sure you don't have room for a piece of pie or cake?"

"Oh, no." Joy removed her hands from his and patted her stomach. "I was almost full after that mixed green salad and *delicious* she-crab soup." She barely touched her main course of whipped honey-butter sweet potatoes, lightly seasoned asparagus, and blackened salmon.

"I noticed." Chase chuckled and dabbed the corners of his mouth with a linen napkin. "That's why I asked if you wanted your dinner boxed up. You don't strike me as a big eater."

"Not all at once, no, I'm not. But in another hour or so, I'll be ready for round two." She winked.

Chase grinned as Joy quietly laughed. "Well, we can have the dessert boxed up too and eat it at my place later," he offered. "I'd love to show you where I live."

"Um, where do you live?" she questioned, slightly narrowing her eyes. "I hope not too far away."

"No, about fifteen minutes from here." Chase rattled off his full address to put her completely at ease. "So, maybe twenty minutes or so from your place. I promise to have you home at a respectable hour."

Joy contemplated his offer, gauging the vibe of their evening together, and graciously accepted. She excused herself to the restroom and quickly texted Tiana and Michelle to let them know where she'd be, just in case. Whether it was paranoia or just plain old precaution, Joy could admit to herself that maybe she had seen one too many true crime documentaries.

After selecting their choice of desserts, Chase paid the bill and the two of them left the restaurant with the remainder of their meals and a couple pieces of rich textured key lime pie.

"Are you sure you're okay with coming back to my house?" Chase asked Joy as he handed the valet his parking ticket.

Having recognized Chase, the attendant offered to take his packaged bag of food with him to the vehicle as well. Chase handed the stapled bag and a tip to him before turning to Joy again.

"You seemed a little unsure back there." He casually draped his hands in the pockets of his slacks.

"Yes, I'm good," she assured him, clearing stray strands of hair from her face as she nodded. "I trust you."

Those words rung true. Beyond the luxurious vehicle he drove and the extravagant first date they were enjoying, it was the genuine warmth in his smile and the sincerity behind his words that left an indelible mark on her memory.

"I'm going to take my turn at the restroom." Chase showed Joy to a bench nearby. "The valet drivers look a little backed up, so I'll probably be back before he does."

Joy smoothed her dress beneath her as she sat and smiled at him. "Oh, don't rush on my account. I'm okay."

Chase leaned in closer, certain that she wouldn't pull away, and lightly kissed her soft cheek. "I won't be long," he quietly whispered in her ear. He gently touched her bare shoulder, sure of their attraction, before walking back inside the hotel.

Joy smiled to herself, feeling more appreciated than she had in a long while. The apprehension she held because of his race seemed so insignificant now. They shared more in common than she thought with each passing moment. Joy anticipated the possibility of seeing him again, and their date wasn't even over yet.

The humidity of the day spilled over into the early evening. Joy stood and paced the short sidewalk, eager to catch a light breeze. She rotated her neck to stretch from the strenuous workout she had endured the night prior. Despite her mild jog on the treadmill this morning, her muscles were still slightly sore, although not completely tight. Just as she started back toward the bench, Joy heard a familiar voice call her name.

"Hey, Joy," the man repeated, this time in a softer tone as he got closer to where she now stood.

Joy turned around, visibly shaken by Rico's presence. She tightened the clutch bag in her hand and held up the other to stop him in his tracks.

"I was on my way to your house and saw you from the stoplight." His haircut was shorter than it was when she last saw him, his goatee was trimmed with straight edge lines, and his clothes were new, sharper than any other outfit she'd seen him wear in a while. "What are you doing here? One of your friends having a party again?" he questioned.

Despite his best efforts to impress her, Joy's face was etched with a mixture of concern and contempt. "Rico, I told you that it was over." Her voice was low, but the tone was sharply tart. "I don't know why you flew all the way back from California. You're not staying at my place. I blocked you for a reason."

"So this past year has meant nothing to you?" Rico took a step back and grunted under his breath. "You know we're good together."

"Rico, please leave." Joy's eyes skirted away from the patrons who were also waiting for a valet driver to return with their vehicles. "Don't cause a scene," she whispered.

Rico noticed her discomfort with him and soon realized that she was not there for another banquet or graduation celebration. "So, it's really like that, Joy? Dinner with somebody else,

I guess. Boy, that didn't take long." He scanned her body from head to toe. "I'll give it to you though, that dress is banging."

Joy instinctively smoothed the dress against her body as Chase neared them both. "Yes, it is, and she wore it for me tonight."

"What?" Rico watched as Chase calmly placed his hand on the small of Joy's back, noting that she didn't push him away. "Wait, is this why you've been blowing me off?" Rico glared at Chase and then laughed. "Man, you're not even in her stratosphere. You are straight up wasting your time. Why don't you leave, and I'll take her home." Rico took a few steps towards Joy and grabbed her hand.

Joy snatched away and glared at him. "Rico, stop it! Why don't *you* just leave?"

Chase stepped up, edging Joy behind him. "I believe the lady asked you to leave."

"*I believe the lady asked you to leave,*" Rico mocked him. "Whatever, I'm not talking to you!" Then, out of nowhere, he swung at Chase.

Joy screamed as Chase blocked Rico's fist with a sharp upward motion of his arm. Chase quickly brought him to his knees with a brisk hand chop to the side of his neck. Within seconds Rico was down on the pavement, writhing in pain. The valet drove up in Chase's vehicle as more bystanders looked on, some with their cell phones drawn.

"Get security," Chase instructed the valet, who then radioed the front desk. He turned to Joy who appeared startled and asked, "Are you okay?"

"Yes, I, I, I'm fine," Joy stumbled over her words. "*Oh my God...*" She covered her mouth with quivering fingers and backed up as two security guards rushed to where Rico was on the ground.

Chase turned away from her and spoke briefly with the security guards as bystanders corroborated his account. Moments later, Rico was briefly attended to by onsite staff, handcuffed by the local police, and then promptly led away in a squad car. Chase escorted Joy to his vehicle, which had been relocated by the hotel staff to a parking spot. He opened the passenger door for her and then got behind the wheel. At first, neither of them spoke a word.

"I'm sorry," they both blurted.

"No, you go first." Chase gestured for her to speak.

Joy exhaled, absorbing the dampness of her cheeks with a napkin from her purse. "I'm sorry that happened."

"Who was that clown?" Chase questioned.

Hesitant to answer, Joy sighed, "My ex." She loathed admitting that she even knew him, let alone having dated him. All sorts of thoughts rampaged through her mind about how Chase would view her now, and if he would even want to date her given what had just happened.

"Are you still seeing him?" Chase carefully asked, turning to look her in the eyes. The expression on his face seemed to ask more.

"No, I'm not. It's nothing like that." Joy exhaled heavily as she swiped her hair behind her ears. "I broke up with him before you and I even met. It was not good." She sucked her teeth, feeling embarrassed, angry, and hurt all at the same time. "It's a long story."

Chase briefly looked away at the patrons passing on the street before turning back to her. "Would you like me to take you home now?" he reluctantly asked with his body language suggesting the complete opposite.

"No," she answered, determined to not let Rico ruin things between them. Although she was sure Chase's impression of her had changed, Joy did not want such a beautiful night to end that way. "It's a long story, but I would like to tell you about it."

"Okay." Chase nodded and softly smiled at her. He lightly touched her arm with a single stroke of his finger and added, "I'm here to listen."

Chapter Thirteen

PERFECTLY SITUATED IN THE heart of town, the new portrait studio boasted a blend of style, class, and practicality. As the weeks of summer collapsed into fall, Wynter had successfully transformed a drab old storefront with hundreds of square feet into a retreat of southern charm. Joy was invited to work at the official grand opening where she was entrusted with the task of showcasing graduation packages in their booming college town.

The pair worked well together as Joy absorbed more of the business aspect of her blossoming passion. Whether it was consulting with fellow classmates about their ideal choice of in-studio versus on-location venues or couples wanting to memorialize their relationships, Joy welcomed the opportunity of partnering with her former professor. Wynter had pitched the idea of securing contracts with the local high schools for senior and prom photos and shared with Joy the expansion proposals for the future. Expansion that included her as a full-time photographer after graduation.

Joy was elated at the proposition to work with her former professor, especially considering the vast pool of talent from which Wynter could have selected. With so many students eager to be associated with the award-winning Wynter Sommers, it was a no-brainer for Joy. She had already established roots in Simpson, and now in an exclusive relationship with Chase, Joy was firmly set on residing here after graduation.

Chase Carson Carlington... Joy doodled his name on the top sheet of a yellow-ruled notepad in her office. She exhaled at the reality of the two of them being an item, and the notion of them becoming more. It made her smile when she remembered the explanation he gave behind his name, "My mother just had a fascination with the letter C," he had said. Later that night after the fiasco with Rico, Chase and Joy shared more serious moments as she poured her heart out to him about the dysfunctional relationship with her ex.

She admitted to ignoring one red flag after another. Rico was not reliable, respectable, or responsible, but Joy figured one day he would eventually become those things. Chase listened and didn't pass a condemning verdict on her past decisions. He openly shared that he had made plenty of his own mistakes when it came to women.

Although weeks later, Joy could hardly believe the photo on her computer screen—but there it was—Rico in an orange jumpsuit with a purple bruise on his neck. Initially, she felt responsible for Chase getting involved in her ex-boyfriend drama, but as he put it, *he brought that on himself.* Joy hated that Rico now had a simple assault misdemeanor on his record, but she was glad that the situation prompted him to go back to California and leave her alone for good.

"Hmm, orange is not his color," Tiana said as she peeked over Joy's shoulder at the computer screen. "I would've paid money to have seen Chase set him straight." She chuckled.

"Trust me, it was over before it started." Joy shook her head as she closed the computer screen and scribbled over the doodling on her yellow-ruled notepad. "I still can't believe he did that."

"Well, he asked for that spanking, and Chase delivered on the request." Tiana laughed before folding a stick of chewing gum into her mouth.

"Tee, that's not funny." Joy grimaced as she stood from her swivel chair and walked across the room to retrieve printer paper from the bottom cabinet of her built-in bookshelf. "I never wanted anybody fighting over me."

"Girl, are you still thinking about those haters on social media? Listen, they will make a mountain out of a molehill. Just get offline for a while and those trolls will go away."

"I know, but I wasn't trying to get negative publicity for his business. You remember that news clip." Joy sucked her teeth and shook her head. "It was like déjà vu from that accident I had in high school. You remember how hard they came down on Ma, being District Attorney and all, because of me. Reporters dragged her name in the media because *I* decided to text and drive. I'm not trying to do that to him. I don't want to cause any drama in his life, or lost sales from his business, because of my connection to Rico."

"I'm sure he knows that, Joy. Besides, he was protecting you. The video speaks for itself. The tags I've seen online show how much people liked what he did. They were calling him things like *knight in shining armor* and *hero*." Tiana tried convincing her until she saw the distressed expression on Joy's face. "What is it?"

"It's not the fact that he defended me, it's the fact that he defended a *black* woman." Joy shot her a stare that promptly reminded Tiana about the two social media messages she had received from an underground hate group. "If they came at me like that, I could only imagine what they're sending him."

Tiana sat down and quietly watched as Joy loaded paper in the printer. The day the messages showed up in her account, they both felt helpless when the police told them there was nothing they could do. Against Tiana's advice, Joy refused to share those messages with Chase. Since he didn't report getting similar threats, she chose to keep the matter to herself.

"I'm finally happy, I mean *really* happy with someone I'm dating and now to have to deal with this." Joy shoved the paper tray back in the printer and grunted.

"Joy, you do not have to listen to them," Tiana reminded her. "They're DM'ing you, hiding behind a fake name because they're so scared that people will find out who they are. Block them like you blocked Rico and move on. Don't let them run your life."

"Yeah, I know. It's just frustrating to not know who's doing it. If they didn't mask their real IP address, then maybe the police would do something. But the officers here are not trying to investigate this. Somebody would have to break my door down for them to do something."

Tiana groaned from that sad fact. Their experience with the police force back home in Lewiston Springs was totally different from the department currently in Simpson. For them back home, over the generations, people had come to recognize the problem in society for what it was: a pure lack of human morality. In Simpson, the mere color of a person's skin practically drove the economic status in this part of the state. Many residents who were white often had more financial opportunities than those of other races. The political landscape contributed to their reality, but both Joy and Tiana hoped that inequalities in Simpson would become a thing of the past just as they had in their hometown of Lewiston Springs.

Outside of the college dorms and residences within miles of it, there were very few communities with a mixture of different races. It was like night and day where people lived on the outskirts of town. As a result of the many activists in the area seeking to transform the landscape of the city, they encountered pushback from powerful individuals who were resistant to change.

Their conversation was interrupted by the chime from Joy's phone, causing her to quickly look away from Tiana. It was Chase reminding her that she owed him some time at his place after cancelling earlier in the week. Joy had a test to study for and after the mediocre grade she got on a recent pop quiz, she told him that they couldn't meet until she pulled that grade up.

"I can guess who that is," Tiana said with a smirk, raising an eyebrow at Joy.

"Yes, it's Chase. I want to hang out with him, but if Ma finds out that my grades are slipping, I'd never hear the end of it. Especially this close to the end."

"It was only one quiz grade," Tiana emphasized by raising her forefinger. "You can pull that up like that." She snapped her skinny fingers.

"I know, but I have to pass this class. I like hanging out with Chase, but he can be a big distraction." Joy shook her head, recognizing how her boyfriend's antics were constantly drawing her attention away from schoolwork.

"Have him study with you," Tiana suggested.

"We've tried that before and ended up pillow fighting." Joy grinned and playfully rolled her eyes.

"*What*?" Tiana chuckled.

"He kept sneaking behind me and putting a feather in my ear. By the time I realized that it was him, and not a gnat, I had hit myself like three times." Joy chuckled as she recalled. "After I smacked him with a sofa pillow, we ended up pillow fighting. He just likes to play a lot. The only time he was serious was when I did his photo shoot for those new headshots."

I will let you study this time. I promise. Joy received another series of texts from Chase. *Just not during the dinner break while watching Jeopardy! We have to settle this tiebreaker.*

Joy grinned, remembering how he evened their score by correctly identifying Alonzo Clayton, a black man born in Mississippi, as the youngest jockey to ever win the Kentucky Derby. They would keep score of how many questions they correctly answered first before the contestants on the game show buzzed in to respond.

"Is that him?" Tiana asked as Joy looked up from her screen with a smile on her face.

"Yes, it's him." Joy looked down again at her phone to a series of praying hands and heart emojis. "He is such a sweetheart, though."

"Well, on that note, I have to get to class." Tiana picked up her crossbody bag from the storage bench near the bookshelf and waved at Joy. "Catch ya later, girl. And tell Chase I said hi."

"I will. Bye, girl." She waved at Tiana and was soon left alone.

Joy glanced over a paper she had finished revising the night before and submitted it to a professor who taught one of her core classes. She double-checked the syllabi for her other classes, ensuring that no other assignments were due that week. After toying with the idea of meeting her boyfriend for a study date, Joy caved to his offer and gave him a call.

THE FLOOR OF THE workshop was littered with piles of wood shavings and layers of sawdust. Chase turned off the circular saw and removed his safety goggles and respirator mask. He checked the time on the wall and noticed that Joy was due to arrive soon. He snatched off his gloves and quickly swept the floor of the workstation.

"Mr. Carlington, there's someone here to see you." Malcolm stood at the entrance of the shop holding a clipboard at his side.

"Oh, she's right on time." Chase quickly emptied the full dustpan in a nearby trash can and rested the broom against a wall. He pulled off his waxed canvas apron and brushed particles of dust from his arms. "Did you show her to my office like I asked?" Chase washed his hands at a sink in the corner and then walked across the floor where his store manager stood beside the door.

"It's your dad," Malcolm answered as he repeatedly clicked the top of a pen with his thumb. "And yes, he's waiting in your office."

My dad? Chase dragged his hand down across his mouth. At three-fifteen on a Thursday afternoon, Phil could often be found having a leisurely cocktail at the exclusive club he frequented with a hand-rolled cigar. It was his chosen prelude to a three-day weekend he had adopted since squaring things on the ranch. With Travis and his friend as regular stable hands now, alongside the others, things had been running smoothly with Booker at the helm.

"Has he been here long?" Chase looked down at his phone and noticed the missed call from Joy.

"No, just a few minutes." Malcolm's brows furrowed as he sighed. "He did seem a little agitated, though."

Chase grunted under his breath as he divided his attention between his employee and the missed texts from Joy. "Tell him I'll be right there."

"Sure thing." Malcolm nodded and walked back through the breezeway that connected the store from the workshop into the rear door of the main building.

Chase quickly read Joy's messages about her being stuck in traffic due to a fender bender between two other vehicles on the highway.

Take your time and be careful, he texted her.

Always, Joy quickly replied. *They're clearing the roads now. Putting my phone away. Be there soon.*

Chase realized that was going to be Joy's last update to him because she was a stickler for not texting and driving anymore. He finished clearing the dust particles from his pant legs and quickly walked to his office where he found Phil reclining behind his desk with his feet propped up.

"Dad, what are you doing here?" Chase asked as he closed the thick frosted glass door encased in a white wooden frame behind him.

"This is a nice little set-up you have here." Phil rocked in the chair, glancing around the room. "I see you've spruced up the place since my last visit."

"Yeah, a lot can happen in a year." Chase followed Phil's eyes as they bounced from corner to corner. "So, what brings you by?"

"I haven't seen you at the house lately." Phil picked up one of three wooden ornament slices, oddly shaped with jagged edges, that rested near a stapler on Chase's desk.

"I've been busy." Chase folded his arms across his chest, watching as his father held the ornament Joy had proudly made with him during her first visit to his workshop.

"Yeah, I know you have." Phil rotated the ornament in his hands, staring at it strangely. "I heard about that spectacle at LaGrange a few weeks ago." His eyes soon landed back on his son.

"Okay." Chase was stoic. "I didn't do anything wrong. What about it?"

"Let's just say that it didn't go over too kindly that the president of United Sons of Simpson has a son fighting over one of ... *them*." Phil proudly boasted about his exclusive, racially segregated club and proceeded to launch a series of derogatory insults. "I mean, I can understand you wanting them young, but does she have to be black?"

"Dad, I'm not doing this with you," Chase warned, careful to keep his voice lowered in his place of business, as he glared at his father.

"Now, son, I know how much you care about these people," Phil said dismissively in reference to the African American community. "Ever since you were a boy, hanging around with

Travis and the rest of them, it seemed as if you were alienating your own kind."

"*Alienating my own kind?*" Chase frowned. "Treating people like human beings is not alienation. Just because I didn't want to be with Karen, you take that as some kind of insult against the entire white race."

"That girl was right for you." Phil grunted and tightened his lips.

"No, her family's money and connections were right for you!" Chase abruptly shouted, unable to restrain himself.

"Now you watch your tone with me!" Phil pointed at his son as he sprung to an upright position in the chair. He angrily pounded his fist on the desktop, firmly planting his feet on the floor. "You don't want to get on my bad side. I'm warning you, do not bite the hand that feeds you."

His choice of words left Chase baffled. He had long since acquired his own fortune, lived in his own home, and ran his own business. It was ludicrous for his father to have the gall to threaten him.

It wasn't until he heard Phil revive his past threat by saying, "Remember, that winning horse of yours is still on my land," that he understood exactly where he was coming from.

"I can pay you to board her. That's not a problem." Chase's jaw tensed.

Phil stood and walked around the desk to where Chase was. "I don't need your money, son. I want your respect. Now, either you stop making a fool of me by running around with that gal or you can find somewhere else to take your filly, and the others too."

"But Dad, she's in the middle of training and—"

"No, that's it," Phil growled. "Dump the gal or Impartially True and your other two horses are put out. And don't even think about taking them to Dixon's farm. They won't accept them. So, either do as I say or get ready to ship those precious horses of yours out of this county." Phil eyed Chase with a menacing smirk, daring him with unspoken words.

Chase's jaw tightened as he returned an equally resentful glare. "I'll move them then." He was steadfast in his conviction and unmoved by his father's threat as he opened the door to his office. "I'll have them all out of there in a couple of weeks."

Phil casually tossed the wooden ornament with the words *Solus Christus* onto Chase's desk as he walked to the threshold of the door. "You got a couple of *days*, or I'm filing an eviction notice."

Chase slammed his office door shut behind Phil as he walked away. He grunted through clenched teeth, struggling to contain his anger. On the closed-circuit security monitors, he watched as Phil cavalierly exited the front doors of the store and got inside his prized Bentley Continental, a recent addition to his collection of luxury vehicles. Soon, the taillights of his father's car illuminated just before he exited the parking lot.

As Chase was about to turn away from the monitors, he spotted the front of Joy's Acura. He stood motionless and released a long, calming breath to quell the anger bubbling inside of him. He then grabbed his keys, turned the lights off in his office, and met her outside.

"Hey, you," she greeted him as they met at the front of her car. "I thought you were working until four today." Puzzled, she glanced at her wristwatch. "It's only three-thirty."

"I was going to, but I can come in a little earlier tomorrow to finish what I was working on." He wrapped his arms around her and kissed her temple. "How about a change of plans? After I help you study, I want us to go somewhere."

"Chase, I don't know about that." Joy squinted suspiciously at him. "I'm familiar with your study habits…"

He smiled, gently taking the tips of her fingers into his hands. "No, seriously, I'll help you. No distractions." His facial expression transformed, dissolving into a more serious one.

Reading an unusual somberness in his mood, she questioned, "What is it?"

"Would you like to go to church tonight? It's just been one of those days."

"Oh, okay." Joy glanced down at her attire: a white T-shirt, pink athletic capris with pockets, and soft cushioned thong flip-flops.

"Don't worry about what you're wearing." He rubbed her shoulders. "Remember what the pastor said in his sermon last Sunday, *come as you are.*"

"I remember." Joy nodded.

The first time she accompanied Chase to church, the same place where his sister was a fellow member, Joy was welcomed like family. From the moment she stepped inside, the people greeted her with kindness and warmth. It was just as Patricia had described, filled with people from many different backgrounds. She saw several of her classmates there and a couple of professors too. Being that she had visited another church her brother Zachary had attended while he was a student, where she was now a regular, Joy never considered any of the others in the area when she herself became an undergraduate at the university. She just adopted it as her own after moving to the city.

"What time does it start?" Joy asked.

"Six-thirty," Chase answered, his voice filled with hope that she would accompany him. "Will that give you enough time to study?"

"Oh yeah, plenty." Familiar with the mid-week service at his church being dedicated to prayer, praise, and worship, Joy searched his eyes for clues about what could have happened in the span of time between when they had texted each other and her arrival. "Is everything okay?" she quietly asked.

"It will be." Chase's brows furrowed as he looked out at the busy highway. "We'll talk about it later." He let out a deep sigh as his pensive gaze softened. "Ready to follow me out?"

"Well, I was going to see if I could find a nice present in your store for my parents." Joy glanced behind him through the windows of his gallery. "My siblings and I are planning a party. Their thirty-fifth wedding anniversary is coming up, and I just want it to be memorable. You know, sort of a keepsake gift. But it can wait."

"Why didn't you tell me?" Chase playfully thumped her arm with the tips of his fingers, eliciting a smile from her. "Thirty-fifth, huh? Emeralds. You know, I can design a frame, complete with emerald gemstones to commemorate the occasion, and you could take a photo of them at their party to go inside."

"That's a great idea, Chase!" Her eyes lit up as she excitedly bounced in place. "Why didn't I think of that?"

"I don't know, maybe because you were trying too hard to think of something when the answer was right in front of you all along." Chase carefully cleared the feathered bangs from her eyes.

"I think you're right." Joy slipped her hands into his, and softly echoed, "It was right in front of me ... all along."

Chapter Fourteen

"I SURE WAS SORRY to see Impartially True and the others go." Travis looked on as Chase took several trips back and forth from the stable to his pickup truck. "I heard what happened between you and your dad."

"I'm sure if it came from my father, you've only heard part of the story." Chase grunted, clearing out the area his horses had occupied.

"Probably." Travis grinned, walking alongside Chase as he moved about. "Is it true that you won't be on the ranch anymore?"

"More than likely. At least for the time being." Chase tossed gear, supplies, and materials one by one on the back of his truck. "But I'll manage. With God's help, this too shall pass."

As Chase cleared the whips, saddles, and reigns from the hooks on the wall near his horses' stalls, he noticed the familiar scent of hay and leather, reminding him of the countless hours he had spent there. It was only now that he was beginning to grasp the gravity of it all. "Wow, I didn't realize how much stuff

I had here." He released an exasperated sigh before he began loading a bin he had retrieved from his truck.

"Did you need some help?" Travis watched as Chase fought with the wheels of a container stuck in the fringes of a grassy knoll.

"Nah, I'm good." Chase held a hand up to keep him at bay. "I don't want to get you involved in this mess with my dad. You work for him now, not me."

Travis reluctantly took a couple steps backwards and helplessly watched him.

"Booker's been paying the wage we discussed, right?" Chase stood upright after freeing the jammed wheels.

"Yeah, he has." Travis gave a slight nod. "Right on the nose. I haven't had any problems with him."

"Good. Just keep showing up on time and working like you have, and you'll be fine." Chase continued to toss things onto the back of his truck until the last of his personal items had been cleared from the ranch. "Once I get things worked out, would you like to be Impartial's groom?"

Their eyes locked, and a knowing grin spread across both of their faces. There was a silent acknowledgment of the lighthearted banter they had shared earlier, a subtle nod to the contrasting titles given to those who tend to horses, known as grooms, and those who cared for dogs, groomers. Regardless of the title, Travis held a deep appreciation for the honest work he performed.

"You're seriously asking me if I'd like to be her groom?" Travis' eyes lit up. "And travel to all the races in different states?"

"Yeah." Chase cracked a smile.

"Yeah, man!" he bellowed.

"All right, look, I can match your pay, but I have to tell you that the hours will be long on the road, and you'll be seeing more of the trainer than me."

"Not a problem. With Mama's passing, I need to stay busy. Besides, she's got it. Impartial has what it takes to go all the way."

"For sure." Chase nodded. "We got a lot of work ahead, but I'm believing for that big Derby run." He looked back at Travis before hopping in his pickup. "I'll be in touch."

"All right, man." Travis waved to his longtime friend, his face a canvas of both gratitude and respect.

Chase waved back as he drove toward the entrance of the property. Soon the sound of tires crunching on gravel gave way to a lingering trail of dust. As he glanced in the rearview mirror, memories of growing up on the ranch flooded his mind. Despite his sacrifice, Chase knew that the woman he was falling in love with was worth so much more.

"WHERE DID YOU GET that frame?" Margaret chuckled with excitement. "Your father and I are taken aback by all the little details and embossed emeralds. Oh my goodness, it's gorgeous!"

"I take it you got your gift in the mail today." Joy giggled at her mother's excitement as she sat in her home office. She had been expecting a call from her parents ever since she had received a message on her phone, alerting her that the parcel had been delivered to them that morning.

"Hey, Joy!" Gerald's booming voice called out to her as he shared the speaker phone with his wife. "Yes, we got the package not too long ago. Whoever the artisan is did a masterful job."

Upon seeing the finished product, Joy could hardly believe how well Chase had masterfully designed the frame on such short notice. The hours he worked on her project, while keeping the deadlines of paying clients, amazed her. Although she had offered to pay him, Chase adamantly refused to accept any money from her. He instead bargained for her time to accompany him on a weekend getaway after her midterms in the coming days.

"And the photograph came out beautifully!" Margaret exclaimed, complimenting their daughter's skills. "We have the perfect place for it. This is going over the fireplace in the den."

At the dinner party in Lewiston Springs, Joy had announced to her parents, while also notifying her siblings, that her gift for their thirty-fifth wedding anniversary was a photo shoot from her as an official photographer. Though initially apprehensive about sharing her change in dream jobs, Joy's announcement was surprisingly met with excitement from everyone ... except Zachary.

"I like the Scripture inscribed on it – Ephesians 5:28, the emeralds – in my favorite shade of green, and the unique design that has so much detail. I just like the whole thing!" Margaret laughed, drawing a hearty chuckle from Gerald too. "And the way you captured us in the photo was just beautiful. The whole evening was wonderful. We were completely caught off guard."

"We didn't suspect a thing," Gerald added. "No clue whatsoever."

Joy smiled at their reaction. It was just tough for her that Zachary hadn't shared in the family's acceptance of her career change as much as she had hoped. Despite everyone's excitement over her new employment opportunities, he remained indifferent, showing no signs of enthusiasm. When Joy met him alone in the kitchen after the wait staff had been relieved for the evening, he shared that he had news of his own.

Unbeknownst to Joy, Zachary had been working to secure opportunities for her in the sports broadcasting industry. Far from angry about her decision, he expressed how blindsided he was that she had changed her mind about the career she was once so passionate about. Zachary had always been her protector, and because he was also the sibling she was closest to, Joy couldn't help but internalize his disappointment. It was not until he eventually disclosed his genuine happiness for her that she felt at ease. Zachary made it clear he would be there to support her in whatever she may need.

"Where did you order it from?" Margaret inquired again about the frame. "A few of my clients might be interested."

"Carlington Home Furnishings." Nervous about revealing her relationship with Chase, Joy closed her laptop and pushed it aside. Apart from not having introduced anyone to her parents before, she had now fallen in love.

"How did you find them?" Margaret asked. "Local advertisement?"

"My boyfriend owns it," she blurted.

"Boyfriend?" Margaret questioned.

"Boyfriend?" Gerald repeated.

"Boyfriend." Joy giggled.

In no time, she found herself bombarded with a barrage of questions about his identity, the story of how they met, and the duration of their relationship. She fielded each question as succinctly as she could, leaving the most obvious detail for last.

"Oh, and he's white." With bated breath, Joy nervously awaited their response, her mind contriving all sorts of different reactions.

After some initial silence, Gerald eventually asked, "Are you sure this is what you want?"

"What do you mean, Dad?" She wondered if he was practicing something different than what he preached. Joy had always known her father to be a fair man, direct in his approach, but thoughtful in his responses. Hearing him ask if this was what she wanted left her a bit confused.

"I think what your father is trying to ask is, are you serious about this relationship?" Margaret's soft tone matched Gerald's, but still the question hit Joy in an offensive way.

"I am," Joy answered, sure of her feelings. "Does it matter that he's white?"

"I'm your father, so naturally I'm going to have questions about any man in your life. As for him being white, I don't care about that. What I care about is if he'll treat you right. Will he protect you?" Gerald paused, sighed, and then grunted. "I get that times have changed since I was your age, but there are still people out there carrying hatred in their hearts for people who look like us."

"Dad, I know that."

"No, Joy, I don't think you do." Margaret's tone was ominous. "That's how Gerald's older sister was killed, for being with a white man."

"*Dad, I'm sorry* ... I didn't know."

"Of course you didn't." Gerald grunted again, and it was obvious to Joy that the pain of losing his sister was still fresh in his mind. "It's not something we talk about. I didn't know everything at the time, being a fourteen-year-old, but I learned enough."

"You mean Aunt Thelma?" she asked, her eyebrows furrowing in confusion. "I thought she accidentally drowned in the lake."

"It was no accident. *He* was beaten up ... *she* lost her life." Gerald almost choked on his words as he relived the past, prompted to draw parallels between his sister's age then and Joy's age now.

"All we're trying to say, Joy, is to be careful." Margaret sighed deeply.

Confronted with her family's past, Joy was now conflicted about her future. She wondered if she was being naïve to think that decades of time had remedied the issues of the past, at least most of them. It was often said that there was more good in the world than bad, especially in the culturally diverse city of Simpson. Her hometown of Lewiston Springs, Mississippi had transformed over the years. She reasoned that if change could happen there, it could happen anywhere.

"I am always careful," Joy assured them both. "Chase is a good person."

"That's his name?" Gerald asked, sounding deep in thought. "Hmm ... *Chase*. Well, I'd like to meet him. You've never introduced us to anyone that I hadn't randomly met at a game when you were in high school. For you to tell us about him, things must've gotten pretty serious."

Things had gotten serious, more serious than she had anticipated. After knowing Chase just shy of three months, Joy found herself enraptured in a fairytale romance. The intimate dinners at his home were nice, their dates on the farm interesting, but their connection of faith was incredible. He pursued every facet of her being. They engaged in deep, lengthy conversations on the phone, enjoyed hours together in person, and spent countless amounts of time in prayer. She believed that she had met her soul mate.

"I'd like to bring him home during the holidays. Once you meet him, I'm sure you'll see what I do."

Gerald and Margaret agreed to Chase spending Thanksgiving with them. Their reservations weren't about Joy's choice in men, but rather how cruel the world could be at times. However, Joy could tell there were burning questions that Gerald was eager to pose to the man he suspected already had his daughter's heart. As a loving father to his baby girl, she knew he was determined to protect her any way he could.

Chapter Fifteen

WHILE TRAVELING ON THE highway towards his residence, Chase and Joy engaged in a playful exchange of flirtatious smiles and elusive glances. There was an undeniable chemistry between them. After hearing a soul-stirring message from a guest speaker during church service this morning, the pair looked forward to spending the rest of their Sunday afternoon together, further discussing the Thanksgiving visit to Lewiston Springs and the plans he had for Christmas that didn't include family.

"Are you sure you're okay with this?" Chase questioned as he pulled into his driveway and parked beside Joy's vehicle.

She looked at him and nodded as he turned the car off. "Of course I'm okay with it. You've had this event planned before you met me."

"I know, but we've, you know, become so close over the past few months. I just feel weird not taking you with me."

"Does it feel weird not being with me?" Joy blushed. Her feelings were mutual.

"More and more each day," Chase admitted, resting a hand on her knee. "Why don't you just change your mind and come with me? It's a showing of my latest pieces to some very influential people in the industry. And tomorrow is the last day to modify my reservation to the event." He searched her eyes for a hint that she would forgo the Christmas festivities with her extended family to spend it with him in the bustling city with all the fanfare. "Come on, you know you want to spend Christmas in the Big Apple."

Joy toyed with the idea of not going home for Christmas this year, but she wasn't sure that she could trust sleeping in the same bed as Chase again. "Going there sounds nice ... but no."

"Are you sure that it's because of your family, or is it because of last night?" Chase's gaze lingered on her. He traced the curvature of Joy's jawline before gently nudging her chin in his direction. "Nothing happened."

Joy shied away from looking him in the eyes as she fidgeted with her fingernails. "But it almost did." Her strong emotions almost led to a betrayal of the commitment she had to celibacy. There was no other man she held such strong emotions for who also challenged her willpower to abstain. No one. When she found herself in his bed, cuddling after a home movie date, Joy knew that she could never spend the night in his room again.

"But it didn't. We stopped and you slept in the guest room. Stop beating yourself up about something that didn't happen."

"Chase, I'm not beating myself up about something that didn't happen." She squeezed his hand. "I'm frustrated with myself because I *wanted* it to happen."

It was at that moment Chase recognized Joy's pure love for him. He was confident in his feelings for her, but couldn't help but wonder if she felt the same way. Upon hearing her express it, Chase discarded his lingering doubts.

"I'm in love with you, Joy," he quietly admitted to her for the first time out loud.

With a smile forming on her lips, Joy shifted her body towards him and replied, "I'm in love with you too, Chase."

"And I'm sorry." His eyes drifted away from her to the front of his home.

"You're sorry?" Joy stared at him curiously. "For what?"

"For last night." He looked back at her. "I never want to put you in that position again... or myself. I was not planning last night with those intentions in mind." He paused, releasing a cleansing breath. "I'm as serious about celibacy as you are. I've had friends make fun of me, especially in college, because I've never gone all the way with a woman, but the problems in their lives sure weren't convincing me to do it."

"Same here," she admitted. "Trust me, I learned a lot from watching my best friend go through it. She got pregnant after the first time." *Amongst other things*, Joy thought.

"Well, I'm not worried about that because the first person I sleep with will be my wife." Chase gave her a flirtatious wink before stepping out of the vehicle.

Joy blushed, reading the innuendo between his words. Ever since their deep conversation about chastity, a whole new level of trust developed between them as they became completely transparent with one another.

Chase soon opened the passenger door for her as he offered a friendly wave to a neighbor in the distance. The cool breeze of the sunny late November day gently disturbed the loose curls of Joy's hair as she stood on the pavement. Chase retrieved the bag of takeout food from the back seat before he followed his girlfriend along the stone-paved path towards his custom French doors. The exquisitely crafted archway, with its delicate patterns and graceful curves accentuated with hues of blue and gray, enhanced the overall charm of the entrance.

Once Joy plugged in the numbers to unlock the keypad as Chase stood behind her holding the food, she feverishly searched her handbag for her ringing cell, clumsily balancing her Bible tightly gripped in her arms. "Hey, Wynter," she answered, walking inside of his spacious foyer. "Oh, I'm sorry to hear that. Sure, I can do that. No, it's not a problem."

As Chase closed and locked the front door to his home, his eyes lingered on Joy, mesmerized by how the elegant flowy sleeve wrap-style dress accentuated her beauty. He carefully placed his keys in the delicate porcelain tray on the table near the entrance and took the food to the kitchen table that overlooked the open living room.

"Yeah. We just got back from church and were about to have lunch. Give me about an hour. Oh, I'm sure Chase won't mind." She looked over at him and smiled.

Chase took off his suit jacket and tossed it over the back of the sofa in his living room. "What won't I mind?" With an arched brow, he began undoing the buttons on his cuffs.

Joy looked at him and placed her forefinger across her lips, quietly shushing him. "Wynter, stop apologizing, things come up. Okay. I'll see you in an hour." After ending the call, she warmly gazed at Chase.

With his head slightly tilted, he asked, "What is it?"

"That was Wynter."

"I gathered that," Chase smartly replied as he loosened his necktie. "What did she want?" The steely gaze in his eyes hinted at his resistance to compromise on the rest of their plans for the day.

"Well, she had an emergency come up and she needs someone to watch her daughter for a couple of hours while she gets things squared away."

"Why can't her babysitter do it?"

"Chase, it's Sunday and she's tied up this weekend." Joy shrugged as she rested her purse on an end table.

"It's Sunday over here, too." Chase eyed her as his lower back rested against the upper part of the sofa. "We were supposed to spend some time alone. I've only seen you once last week because she had you covering for her and now again today, of all days."

Joy sighed as she pulled off her heels and slid into the comfortable pair of slippers she had left beside the coffee table this morning. She walked over to where he was and stood in front of him. "Look, you're right. I'm sorry. I should've asked you before saying that it was okay." With a tender gaze, she flattened her hand against his loosened necktie. "As a friend, I just wanted to help out. The past few weeks have been pretty rough for her. She's had some personal issues going on and the studio is slammed with more work than we can handle this time of the year."

"Joy," Chase softly said her name as he slid his arms around her waist. "She's supposed to be guiding you, not having you do everything for her. Look, I get that she's this award-winning photographer and everything, and you want to build your clientele, but baby, don't let her use you. Besides, a thirty-something-year-old woman can handle her own personal business without involving you."

The silence in the room spoke volumes. Joy realized that Wynter's name brought in plenty of business, but she had to also value her own worth. Although she was still learning and growing in her craft, Joy understood Chase's perspective. It was important to maintain boundaries when it came to business and personal matters, and not to blur the line between the two.

"Okay, I'll call her back." Joy picked up her cell again and unlocked the screen.

Chase took the phone from her hand and gripped it in his palm. "No, don't. You've already told her that you'd watch her." He sighed, setting the phone aside.

"Are you sure?"

"Yeah, I'm sure," he answered, sliding the tie from around his neck.

"It's only going to be for a little while." Joy slid her hands into his. "And Autumn is a fun two-year old. A little active, but fun," she said, sounding as if she was trying to convince herself. Noticing Chase's obvious disappointment, she soon became despondent herself. "If you don't want her here, I can take her home and watch her there."

"No, it's fine," he tried to convince her. "She can come over."

"No, I think it's better that I just watch her at home." Joy's eyes drifted to their hands where he had intertwined their fingers. "Besides, it's closer to where she lives."

Chase let out a frustrated sigh, his shoulders slumping. "So, how long will you be watching her?"

"She asked for a couple of hours."

"Okay. I can just stop by your place a little later." Chase picked up his suit jacket and gazed at Joy as she picked up her purse and headed for the guest room. "And Joy?" When he called her back, there was a distinct warmth in his voice.

"Yes." She turned around and faced him as she stood at the threshold of the guest bedroom.

"I'm sorry for coming at you like that." As he apologized, his eyes softened with genuine remorse.

"It's okay, we've quashed it." Joy softly cleared her throat before giving a gentle smile.

"I know," he quietly began, his eyes searching hers for understanding. "I was just looking forward to some alone time before we leave in a couple days to visit your family. You have classes tomorrow, I need to wrap things up at the store, and then we both need to pack. I probably won't see you again until Tuesday."

"I'll try to stop by tomorrow," she promised him. "But we'll have plenty of time together there."

"It won't be the same and you know it. Your dad will probably be giving me the side eye the whole time I'm there." Chase smirked. "To tell you the truth, I'm a little nervous about meeting him."

"You talk like he's some mafia kingpin." Joy chuckled as she walked inside of the guest bedroom and sat on a chair overlooking his spacious backyard.

Chase followed her and stood in the doorway with his jacket neatly folded over his arm.

"My dad is cool, really, he is." Joy rummaged through the overnight bag for her favorite pair of jeans and round neck long-sleeve shirt.

"But you told me that he has some questions for me." Chase's face flushed with embarrassment as he rested his shoulder against the door frame.

"You are so overthinking this." Joy draped her clothes on top of the comforter spread across the bed. "Listen, my father actually reminds me a lot of you."

"So, he's a really cool white guy with a great body?" Chase opened his arms and struck a pose.

"Ew!" A scowl spread across Joy's face as she teasingly hurled a pillow in the shape of Alabama from the bed towards him. "Don't ever make me get a visual of my dad as having a great body."

Chase laughed as he tossed the pillow back onto the bed. "You're right. That probably wasn't a good visual for you."

Joy shook her head as their laughter gradually faded. "Anyway, my advice for you when you meet him is to just be yourself. He will love you." She met him in the doorway and gently caressed the sides of his face.

"You think so?" Chase's voice softened as he steadied his eyes on her.

"Well, you already know that I do," Joy quietly answered, allowing her arms to rest comfortably around his neck. "I'm sure that he will too."

———— ◆ ————

"It's officially been six weeks without any alcohol," Lucille bragged about her sobriety to Chase as she busied herself in the kitchen. "Not even my Alabama Bramble." Ever since

Patricia had her baby last month, Lucille had been determined to make a fresh start for her new grandchild.

"That's wonderful, Mom. Thursday should be great with Pat, Paul, and the new addition. A new holiday and a new beginning, right?"

"That's right, it sure will. But why does it have to be without you? Are you really going out of town for Thanksgiving?" Lucille dried the sides of a glass Irish coffee mug with a paper towel. "But we always have dinner together. What makes this year any different?" She slid the tall decorative mug across the kitchen counter to him and folded her arms.

"Joy." The mention of her name was met with an expression that defied explanation. "I'm meeting her family at the end of the week."

"*Oh...*" Lucille smiled as Chase raised the mug of his favorite winter beverage from childhood: a cup of hot chocolate garnished with whipped cream and bits of peppermint chips.

"Yeah, I'm driving to Mississippi with her to meet her family." With a subtle grin, he leaned back in his chair and leisurely sipped his drink.

It was quite a pleasant surprise when he brought Joy over to meet her several weeks ago, at a time when Phil was conveniently out of town. Midterms were over and Chase and Joy were fresh from a weekend excursion to the Yucatán peninsula of Mexico. The all-inclusive resort left Joy breathless. Chase had set up a romantic date, complete with a sunset walk on the white sandy beach. It was followed by a private dinner on their hotel terrace where they indulged in flavorful, authentic Mexican cuisine.

"How long do you plan on staying in Mississippi?" Lucille grinned.

"Four days." Chase emphasized his point by holding up four of his fingers. "But not everyone will be there. Just her parents and one of her sisters. Her other siblings are supposed to come home for Christmas."

"Does she have a large family?" Lucille inquired.

"If you count all of the in-laws, I guess you could say that."

"In-laws?" Lucille sought clarification. "You're talking as if you want to marry this girl."

Chase reached into his pocket and pulled out a velvet box. He opened it and revealed the diamond ring inside. "Mom, I do."

Lucille cupped her hands over her mouth. After the initial shock of seeing the diamond glisten under the recessed lighting, she held her arms open to her son. "*Oh, Chase, I'm so happy for you!*" She walked around the counter and hugged him. "Joy is going to adore this ring." Lucille rested a hand over her chest as she held the ring up with the other. "This is just beautiful."

"Thanks, I think she'll like it." He carefully placed the ring back inside of the velvet-lined box and set it on the stone countertop. "I ordered it custom-made a couple weeks ago and picked it up from my jeweler on the way over here."

"When do you plan on asking her?" Lucille sat on a stool next to him.

"I don't know." He exhaled heavily. "I want her family to know me first, just like how you know her. That's very important to Joy. And I want to get to know them as well." He gazed at the ring securely nestled inside of the box, reminiscing about the times he had brought her to the farm before he was forced to leave. Knowing how hard his father was, even before he was banned from the ranch, it had been difficult maneuvering around Phil's schedule. And now with his horses boarded just over the state line, Chase couldn't bring himself to explain to Joy the reason why.

"Where is she today?" Lucille smiled as she rested her hand on Chase's arm, her eyes fixed on the sparkling diamond cluster in the box. "You usually spend Sundays with her now."

"We were together earlier at church, but now she's doing someone a favor by watching her child for a couple hours."

"Oh, okay."

"And how was your day?" Chase inquired, figuring by the empty dishes piled in the sink and scent of lingering food in the air that she had company.

"You know, the usual. Your father and I had oatmeal and bran muffins for breakfast washed down with a little filtered black coffee. Although he did prefer to have it with almond milk this morning." Lucille rattled off Phil's diet as if she was reading from a notepad for their resident doctor. "He's been watching his cholesterol and blood pressure, but you and I both know your father could stand to walk around the track a few times a week."

"Don't I know it." Chase let out a tired sigh as he picked up a red velvet cupcake from the revolving carousel holder in the center of the island and took a generous bite. "Why do you have these desserts hanging around?" The cream cheese frosting clung to his fingers as he carefully placed the dessert on a square orange napkin.

"That's your aunt's fault. Virginia brought half a dozen here so she could get them out of her house. She had a book club meeting last night and one of the ladies picked up a dozen for six members. Well, she didn't want them spending the night in her house, so she dropped them off last night." Lucille spoke of the cupcakes as though they were disruptive children coming for a dreaded sleepover. "I hid them in the oven from Phil and after he left the house a few hours ago for a club meeting, I set them out, hoping to get rid of them before he comes back." She chuckled. "I've asked Pat to talk to him about his weight. She has a way of getting through to him, being his only daughter and all."

"Yes, she does." Chase nodded as he enjoyed another mouthful of the moist dessert.

"There's only two left now, maybe Joy would like one," his mother offered.

"She won't eat them." Chase smiled. "She's made it clear that she's saving her extra calories for Thanksgiving." He chuckled, reflecting on her strict exercise regimen.

"I can understand that. She has a lovely figure." Lucille chuckled. "Anyway, we went on to church and had an early dinner afterwards. Booker joined us here at the house for a little while since Pat and Paul stopped by with the baby before going on home."

"Oh yeah? How have things been working out lately? I mean with Booker. I haven't spoken to him in a while."

"Pretty good." She gave a confident nod. "He's got his own place now, back on your father's good side," she gently smiled, "and doing well. It kind of feels like old times again, except for you not being here."

"Mom, I've told you, I have nothing to say to Dad." Chase wiped the residual frosting from his mouth and then his fingers after finishing the cupcake. "If you heard the things he said about Joy..."

"I know, son. I know. Probably nothing I haven't heard him say about Dinah when she was alive." Lucille resignedly sighed. "I just hope this thing with the horses hasn't driven a wedge between you two forever."

"This is not just about the horses, Mom, and you know it."

"I know, honey. Joy is always welcomed here as far as I'm concerned."

"Do you really think I'm going to bring her back here with him around?" He glared at her. "Not happening. I didn't feel right bringing her here when he was out of town the last couple of times, and I don't feel right hiding her from him either. It's just not right. I had to call you today just to make sure he wasn't here before coming over to avoid dealing with him."

"He didn't care for my friendship with Dinah either, but we found a way. Prenup or not, she was still my friend." Lucille sighed and tapped her fingers on the counter. "That's just who he is. At sixty years old, I doubt if he's changing anytime soon."

"And that's okay with you?" Chase stared at her and narrowed his eyes. He couldn't bear to listen to his mother any longer as she continued to justify his father's actions. In that moment, something inside of him snapped.

"I never said that it was okay, Chase," she clarified. "But I married that man for better or worse, and those vows are sacred to me."

"Your vows are sacred? What does marriage mean to you?" With a curious expression, Chase spontaneously peppered her with questions. "Are you happy? I mean, really, when is enough going to be enough, Mom? Your best friend was a black woman, and you didn't even go to her funeral!"

The mood in the room abruptly changed as Chase's outburst rendered Lucille speechless. What had begun as a normal conversation suddenly morphed into an intense and heated exchange.

"I didn't say anything about it before because I thought you really were that broken up over her passing that you couldn't bear to see her in that coffin. Thinking about the way Dad gave me an ultimatum about my horses, I now see that he must've given you the same decision to make when it came to Dinah. It didn't click until you mentioned that prenup again. You found a way to downplay it like you always have, refusing to stand up to who he is." As he paused, a heavy silence thickened the tension in the room. "Am I right?"

Lucille's lips parted, but she was unable to utter a single word.

"I know you signed a prenup, but money isn't everything." Chase snatched the box with the ring in it from the counter and snapped it closed. He shoved it back into his pocket and stared at his mother. "When you've sobered up about that too, give me a call."

Chase stormed out of the house and slammed the door shut behind him.

Chapter Sixteen

LEWISTON SPRINGS, POPULATION 21,867.

Chase read the engraved wooden sign as he and Joy rode through the entrance of her quaint town. He exhaled and adjusted the collar of his buttoned down long-sleeve shirt that was perfect for the crisp fifty-eight degree day.

"Please don't tell me you're getting nervous." Joy smiled at him as they stopped at a traffic light near a popular walking trail in the heart of the city. "I've told you already, just be yourself and they will love you."

The softness of her voice effortlessly put him at ease. It was no wonder that when she was around him, Chase was calmed by Joy's very presence. He was immediately reminded of why he had given up so much to be with her, and in turn she had shown her devotion by being the first man formally introduced to her family. As they passed various landmarks of her birthplace, Joy pointed out L.S. Central Park, a place that held fond memories for her as a child, as well as the middle school where she formed a lifelong friendship with her best friend, Michelle, and the high school football field where she was honored by being crowned homecoming queen by her peers.

The road leading up to her parents' property was flanked by overhanging oak trees. In excitement, Joy drew Chase's attention to the progress of construction just beyond the wooden stakes on the land. The sight of a crane, excavator, and freshly poured cement marked advancement in the project Margaret was determined to have completed by spring. She longed to establish her own tradition of biannual family reunions, in May and December, with the heirs in her and Gerald's lineage.

"Are you ready?" Joy asked as they sat in her parents' driveway.

"As ready as I'll ever be." Chase looked away from her and toward the movement of blinds at one of the front windows. "Did you see that?"

"I saw it." Joy giggled. "I think that's my sister, Elisha, being nosy. She's supposed to be over here helping Ma get dinner prepped."

"They're cooking already?" Chase curiously questioned.

At first, Joy grinned in response, and then she said, "Yeah. They're probably washing the greens and mixing pie batter to be stored away until tomorrow. Except for one bonus pie that my mother always bakes beforehand."

"Why is that?"

"Well, after you hang around my dad for a while, you'll soon understand why." She grinned. "But mostly they're preparing a meal for you tonight."

"Oh, Joy, they didn't have to go through all of that for me." With his elbow propped on the door frame, Chase wore a soft smile as he pondered their hospitality.

"They know that, but they want to. Just accept it. They're good people."

Chase nodded. "Okay."

"Listen, I think we better get inside before we see more blinds moving at the windows." Joy unbuckled her seatbelt and collected her purse from the floor beside her feet.

Chase looked towards the house, taking in its distinctive rustic exterior, before shifting his gaze back to Joy. "Let's do this." He gently kissed the back of her hand before stepping out of the car. They soon walked hand in hand inside her childhood home and unexpectedly entered an empty foyer.

"Hey, Ma? Dad?" Joy called, knowing they couldn't be too far away. "I'm home!" She clung to Chase's hand as their footsteps echoed through the hallway.

"Oh, hey, Joy! We're back here in the kitchen," Margaret called out to her.

Joy entered the kitchen, and there she met eyes with her parents, Elisha, Tyler, and little Jaxon who ran into her waiting arms. Joy crouched to his level, scooped him up from the floor and kissed him on the cheek.

"Hey, everybody, I want you to meet my boyfriend, Chase Carlington." Joy looked at Chase as she adjusted Jaxon on her hip.

"Hello, it's nice to meet you all." Chase's eyes drifted from one endearing face to the other. He hadn't seen so many smiling faces at once since the last church service they attended on Sunday. As he shook one hand after another, his nervousness faded away.

After multiple conversations, some occurring simultaneously, with those whom he hoped would someday be his in-laws, Chase began to feel at home. It wasn't long before he was enjoying a competitive game of Chess with Tyler in the den area while Gerald lounged in a recliner a couple feet away. Joy peeked at him from the kitchen and smiled to herself as she walked back to the island counter where Margaret and Elisha were.

"He's a really nice guy," Elisha said, complimenting Joy's taste in men. "I think he's going to be Tyler's new best friend."

"I know, right." Joy chuckled as she turned to Margaret. "So, what do you think, Ma? Aside from him mistaking your sweet potato pie for pumpkin, do you like him?" Her eyes drifted to the appetizing dessert that rested on a cooling rack near the double-oven stove.

Margaret glanced at Joy and nodded as she put the finishing touches on the freshly tossed green salad to serve alongside her homemade chicken and dumplings. "I think he's nice too," she answered, though her response was laced with caution.

With a curious expression, Joy turned her attention towards Elisha, her eyebrows furrowing in speculation. She wondered if their mother might have shared some reservations she had about Chase with her sister.

"What is it?" Joy looked back at Margaret with more probing questions in her eyes. "It's the fact that he's white that's bothering you, isn't it?"

Margaret's eyes met Joy's as Elisha rose from her seat and put her crossword puzzle book aside.

"Um, I'm going to check on Jaxon to see if he's up from his nap." Elisha delicately placed a hand on Joy's shoulder before she left the two of them alone in the kitchen.

Joy circled the counter, moving closer to her mother, and quietly repeated, "Is that what's bothering you?"

Margaret released a labored sigh and briefly closed her eyes. "Joy, I've already told you that doesn't bother me. I'm concerned about you and your well-being. I just don't want you to get hurt."

"Chase is good to me." Joy gently placed her hand over Margaret's, prompting her to stop filling the individual ramekins with salad toppers. "You know me, I wouldn't have brought him home if he wasn't."

"I know, Joy."

"So you don't have to worry." Joy paused, carefully lowering her voice. "What happened to Aunt Thelma is not going to happen to me."

Margaret faced her daughter, looking into those innocent doe eyes, dawning the same expression she often had as a little girl, and warmly smiled at her.

"Just please give Chase a chance to prove to you who he really is."

"I already see who he is, Joy." Margaret resumed filling the ramekins. "I think that young man loves you. Really, I do."

Joy blushed, unaware that the chemistry between her and Chase was so noticeable to others.

"But when you told me that you have yet to meet his father and you all live in the same city, that just doesn't sit well with me. He's meeting both your father and I, so, I just hope that *both* of his parents are okay with at least meeting you." Margaret raised a brow, cautioning her daughter as Elisha reentered the room. She finished filling the containers with toppings and soon called everyone to dinner.

The thought had crossed her mind about why Chase's father was always absent when she visited the ranch. And then she pondered the fact that she hadn't been invited back there in weeks. Before her conversation with Margaret, Joy hadn't considered the possibility that maybe something had happened between Chase and his father that may have involved her. But if the ring she found hidden in his dresser drawer when she was helpfully putting away a load of laundry for him last night was any indication that he was going to propose, Joy had decided that she would have to meet his father first. It would put her family at ease, and more importantly, it would put any lingering suspicions she had to rest.

"Hey, you," Chase whispered, nudging her shoulder with his as they sat at the dinner table. "Why are you so quiet?"

"Just thinking." Joy dragged the portions of uneaten pasta around in her bowl with the tines of her fork. "I'm glad you're here." She mustered a smile as she looked into his eyes, hoping the seeds of doubt planted in her mind wouldn't take root.

Discovering the ring in his drawer confirmed what she already knew about Chase's feelings for her, which counted for everything. Still, though Joy's heart echoed his love, she reluctantly considered the possibility that her mother, who carried an innate ability to read people and situations, was right.

"I'm glad to be here. I'm loving your family," he said to her before turning to acknowledge Gerald's offer to watch a couple of old Derby races from Triple Crown winners with him and Tyler in the den. "I'll be right there." Chase turned back to Joy, noticing her preoccupation. "Are you okay? You look like something's on your mind."

"Dad is wanting to know more about horse racing. For him to look those old videos up, he must really like you," she successfully deflected. "Go, enjoy your time with them. I'll catch up with you after I shower and get changed for bed."

"Are you sure?"

"Yes, of course. By that time, I'll be ready for a slice of that pumpkin pie." She winked.

Chase chuckled. "You're not going to let me live that one down, are you?"

"Not a chance." Joy's grin widened, motioning for him to join Tyler and her father for more male bonding.

After sharing with Margaret her intentions for the rest of the evening, Joy left her family downstairs and retreated to her old bedroom. There, she sank to her knees and sought solace in prayer, relying on God's strength to navigate the possible challenges ahead.

Chapter Seventeen

A COUPLE WEEKS INTO the new year, marking her last semester on campus, Joy stared at the old brick buildings and winding sidewalks with a growing sense of nostalgia. Many of the friends she had made over the course of her college years would soon venture out into their chosen careers and travel different paths in life. While she eagerly welcomed the departure of certain classmates, the absence of others would undoubtedly leave a void in her life.

After her last class for the day, Joy anticipated meeting Chase for lunch. It would only be the third time they'd seen each other since the days before Christmas. He left for his trip to New York, and she went home to visit with her family. Despite it being heavily on her mind, Joy refrained from mentioning why he hadn't introduced her to his father.

"So, you're planning on talking to him today about it?" Michelle questioned her best friend as they chatted on the phone, eager to know more details about their relationship.

"Yes." Joy sighed as she sat at the computer in her home office and scrolled through photo images, dropping them into separate digital folders. "I wanted to wait until after the holidays, you know, to give him a chance to introduce me by Christmas, but he didn't."

"Maybe there's a good reason for that."

"What reason, Michelle? I found a ring in his drawer over a month and a half ago, so I know he wants to marry me, but he can't find a day, an hour, or even a minute to get me and his father together in the same room." She grunted, releasing her pent-up frustration. "Is he ashamed of me?"

"Now, Joy, you know that's not true. Chase has never shied away from taking you anywhere. You guys have been just about everywhere your schedules would allow."

"Except in a room with *both* of his parents. What if his father knows something about him that he doesn't want me to find out?" Joy repetitively tapped her fingers on the mousepad next to her computer. "What if he's playing me?" Still feeling somewhat distant from Chase since his visit to New York, Joy couldn't dismiss the slip of white paper she had seen in his cupholder when he returned home.

She noticed the piece of paper that bore the initials SDC along with a mysterious number while at a gas station when Chase was filling up his tank. Before she could investigate the number further, she only had time to memorize the three digits after the area code before Chase stashed it away inside his wallet. It was typical for him to have random numbers lying around, but his evasive response to her inquiry about who the number belonged to was quite unexpected. Not wanting to press the issue further, like she had with several other numbers she had found to be innocent contacts, Joy decided to let it go.

The weeks of December were a wintry blur of finals, social mixers, and drop-in holiday parties. By the time Joy completed her exams, she hadn't seen Chase but twice outside of Sunday services at her new church home. Since he was busy with the holiday frenzy of shoppers cycling through the doors of his gallery, they barely had the time usually spent talking on the phone. Texting had almost become their main form of communication.

"When I met him over Thanksgiving break, he was on point. You remember how those haters from high school were looking at him when we went out that night."

"Yep, I remember," Joy replied, recalling the mean girls from her graduating class. "That night they barely said a word directly to me, but I overheard them giggling about him being white."

"They laughed, but one was bold enough to try him on the sly." Annoyed at their behavior, Michelle released an audible groan. "But he shut it down before it even got started."

"I know, right. Chase was not having any of that." Joy laughed, her smile lingering long after her giggles faded.

"But if he was playing you, would he have given you his phone when your battery went dead?"

"What are you talking about?" Joy's forehead wrinkled in confusion.

"You don't remember when he gave it to you at the movie theater that night?" Michelle questioned, jogging her memory with other details about the evening. "It was right after we sat down before the lights were dimmed."

"Oh, yeah, I remember now," Joy answered with a nod. "I only had his phone for like five minutes."

With smugness in her voice, Michelle said, "Do you know how much damage I can do in five minutes with Justin's phone? Just give me two, and I'd have all the info needed for our next court date."

Joy chuckled in response. "See, I'm not trying to break in his phone to find something on him. Chase gave me his code."

"That's my point, Joy. You're talking all this stuff about how he might be trying to play you and out of your own mouth, you just admitted in so many words that he wouldn't do that." With a click of her tongue, Michelle expressed her disapproval. "Girl, that man does not have time for games. If you saw some of the guys who tried to take me out, you'd sprint back into his arms."

"What if his father is a racist?" Joy speculated, her brows furrowing with curiosity. "What if he's trying to hide me or something?"

"If his father is racist, that's on his father. Clearly, you know that Chase isn't. And as for trying to hide you, we've already addressed that."

Although Michelle had valid points, Joy still held suspicions about Chase's father.

"Look, I get where you're coming from, but if you feel that way just ask him point blank. Stop beating around the bush, waiting on him to say something when you've got a mouth too. If it were me, I wouldn't have waited through Christmas if this thing had bothered me for well over a month. I just couldn't hold my tongue that long. But it's not me, it's you. So, what are you going to do about it?"

Joy sat quietly, deep in thought, reflecting on Michelle's candor. It was clear that she had a decision to make. Unlike with Chase, she discovered that scouring the internet wasn't as effective as when she researched his father. She stumbled upon a social media page solely dedicated to the ranch and a website highlighting their horse-riding and dog breeding services. Despite her efforts, there were no pictures of him to be found anywhere. Chase had mentioned that his name was Phillip, a name he told her that fell to his oldest brother she heard referred to as Booker.

"I'm going to talk to him about it." Joy leveled a stack of papers together and placed them inside of a folder in the file cabinet near her desk. "Since the New Year rush is over, he asked me to meet him for lunch."

"Girl, why didn't you tell me that you had to go?"

"Because we're not getting together for another hour." Joy glanced at the clock on the wall. "But I do have to stop by the studio for a little bit before meeting him."

"Oh, okay. Another consultation?"

"Yeah, but it'll only take about twenty minutes." Joy checked the lens on her camera before carefully securing it in a cushioned bag. "The Italian restaurant where we're having lunch is right across the street."

"Are you going to be able to talk to him like that in a restaurant?" There was a sense of caution in Michelle's voice.

"No, but if I know Chase, *and I know Chase*," Joy chuckled, "he's going to ask me to come back to his house. I'll wait until we're there to bring it up."

"Well, just remember to be straight with him and allow him a chance to explain."

"Oh, of course. I want to hear everything he has to say."

"I know you do," Michelle quipped, her quirky chuckle just above a whisper. "Keep me posted."

"I will."

After Joy ended her call with Michelle, she stared at the framed collage of photos she had taken with her family during Thanksgiving. There was a picture of Elisha, Tyler, and Jaxon, one of her parents, one of her and Chase, and another of all of them together. She smiled, remembering the moment as if it were yesterday.

In the center of the photo collage was a gold-stenciled message that read, *Our First Thanksgiving Together*, captioned with the date. Although Christmas was equally heartwarming, it didn't feel the same since they had spent it apart. Despite Chase's romantic invitation to New York, she insisted on driving home alone. It was a work trip for him, but she just couldn't take the chance of spending the night in the same bed with him again.

Among the picturesque days of autumn last October, when they visited Mexico, it didn't seem to pose an issue sleeping in the same room with each other. However, there was an undeniable evolution in their relationship over the following weeks. Their bond deepened through intimate late-night phone calls, spontaneous dance parties in the privacy of their homes, and competitive trash talk during their video game battles. They were effortlessly in perfect harmony with one another.

Can you take a 2 o'clock consult today? I have another client. A text came in from Wynter. *Hannah called out sick.*

Joy shook her head as she promptly responded, *Sorry, I have a 2:15 and a lunch date right after.*

She grabbed a bottle of water from the fridge and a small bag of air-popped popcorn from her pantry as she waited for Wynter to reply. There was radio silence for nearly ten minutes before she texted her back.

No problem. Worked it out. See you later.

Okay, Joy replied and tossed her phone inside her purse.

Since Chase had motivated her to recognize the value she brought to the studio, Joy was decidedly more focused on her professional growth and less interested in forming friendships in the workplace. She had come to the realization that over the past few months she had shouldered a heavier workload than both Wynter and the other associate photographer. Joy balked at the idea that she was getting the brunt of work for studio portraits and weekend consultations, while they enjoyed lavish destination shoots simply because she was black. Both Wynter and Hannah, blondes with blue eyes, served as a convincing optic.

In retrospect, Joy wondered if that was one reason why Wynter tried to have her sign a non-compete agreement to be valid for three years. The contract aimed to prevent her from competing with Wynter's boutique studio for this specified time if she chose to leave her company. Under this type of agreement, Joy would have also been banned from revealing any trade secrets learned during or after employment in their area. Even though a governmental agency had moved to ban such clauses, to Joy's relief, Wynter failed to get the original contract back she had presented to her when she first began working in her studio months ago. One could relegate that to the busyness of the grand opening coupled with the holiday season, or simply God's ordained covering.

It was still fresh in Joy's memory how angry Chase had gotten when he found the contract in her office the week before their Thanksgiving break. Initially, she didn't view things the same way he had, that was until Wynter started asking her to watch her child. Joy had mistakenly believed they were forming a sincere friendship only to discover she was being used. So many things flooded her mind in hindsight, especially the fact that Wynter had yet to secure or even provide updates about the proposed school contracts, which was a major selling feature to Joy agreeing to work with her. It had become clear that Wynter had ulterior motives and was unashamedly taking advantage of her.

As part of her New Year's goals, Joy had decided to part ways with Wynter and continue with growing her own business. She didn't need someone to take a sizeable percentage of her profits when she was doing just as much, sometimes even most of the work. With Chase's assistance as a successful businessman, she was learning to merge her creative abilities with sound business practices.

Looking forward to our lunch date. Shamelessly bringing my appetite today, Joy read the text from Chase.

Resolved to discuss her concerns about their relationship with him, Joy inwardly struggled with the fear of her mother's worries becoming her own. Cautiously considering Michelle's advice and the concerns of her family with the apparent love in her heart, Joy recognized that it was wise to know the truth before reacting to a version of it.

As she pulled into the parking lot, Joy noticed a vehicle parked in the space normally occupied by Hannah. She parked beside the flashy Bentley Continental, admiring its sleek, polished exterior. Figuring that it must be the client Wynter was busy with that prevented her from taking Hannah's two o'clock consultation, Joy walked inside of the studio to a noticeably empty lobby.

"Oh, hey, Joy." Wynter emerged from the back of the studio. "I heard the door chime. Just wanted to see if it was you." She gently smiled. "Do me a favor. After your client gets here, please put the *Out to Lunch* sign in the window. I'll be tied up for a little bit."

"Okay." Joy looked at the sign that rested beside the front door on a large white pedestal stool, and then back to where Wynter stood. "How long will you be here today?"

Wynter glanced at her watch and casually shrugged. "Maybe another hour or so."

"Oh, okay. Well, I'll be gone by the time you finish up. Did you need anything done before I leave then?"

"Wynter?" The terse voice beckoned from her rear office.

Wynter locked eyes with Joy as she raised a hand to her and answered the man, "I'm coming now. I was just getting my employee settled." Without delay, she vanished into her office.

There was something about her voice in the way she answered him, *I was just getting my employee settled*, as if Joy was a new hire that didn't know anything about the business. Beneath the surface, an unspoken tension simmered as Joy scoffed and headed towards her desk. Upon finishing her consultation, she put the sign in the window and then left for lunch across the street.

Chase was already waiting for her when she arrived. She spotted his pickup truck with splatters of mud on the tires and hubcaps, figuring that he must have just made another trip across the state line in neighboring Georgia. Under any other circumstance, he would never drive his vehicle that filthy. Whenever he went to the ranch across the state line, Chase would always drive his truck, careful to keep his sporty Ferrari away from dirt and gravel roads. He never explained to her the reason why he had moved his prize-winning horse there, and the other two for that matter, but Joy supposed there had to be a good one for him to travel nearly an hour away at least once a week.

"Joy, over here!" Chase waved his hand as he rose from a seat a few feet away from the recently vacated podium at the entrance of the restaurant. Since the hostess had temporarily left her post to seat another couple, Chase ensured that Joy saw their table where he had already placed drink orders.

"Hey, have you been here long?" She hugged him, noticing the crisp scent of his bodywash mingled with the woodsy fragrance of aftershave. "*Mm*, you smell good." Joy supposed he must've worked at his store instead and not been on a ranch after all, possibly filling in for an employee because he smelled nothing like horses or the woodshop as she greeted him.

"Thanks. After that ride this morning, I took a shower at Greenfield's farm before the drive back." He briefly stretched his neck before passing her a menu. "I didn't want to show up here smelling like an animal." He chuckled, perusing the menu placard.

"So, you went to Greenfield's?" Joy's face was filled with confusion as she carefully set the menu on the table and rested her hands against its smooth surface.

"Yeah, I just told you that." Chase continued skimming the options available for dinner portions.

"*Excuse me*?" Joy took his quick response as a sharp one. "What's with the attitude?" Her eyes narrowed at him.

"*Attitude*? What are you talking about? I don't have an attitude." Chase's face crumbled into concern as Joy stood to leave.

Gripping the purse straps on her shoulder, she muttered, "Something's off." Joy stared at Chase, challenging him to admit to whatever he had done. Though they hadn't known each other for long, she knew him very well. "Look, I don't want to do this here, so I'm just going to leave." She glared at him before marching out of the restaurant.

Chase quickly pulled a few bills from his wallet and left it on the table before he rushed out behind her. "Joy, what just happened in there?" He caught up to her in the parking lot and grabbed her hand. "What's going on?" A look of confusion washed over his face as she snatched her hand away.

Joy wedged a finger under her nose as she collected herself. "Do you think I'm stupid?" Her chest heaved as she shook her head in disbelief. "I may be young, but I'm not dumb!"

"Joy, what are you talking about?" His eyes pierced hers as he took a few steps closer. "Please, talk to me."

"You told me that Greenfield farms is not equipped with shower installations." She widened her eyes at him. "You also told me that you hate riding after a hard rain because the track gets so muddy out there. Chase, it rained all the way into central Georgia last night. Did you forget that I watch the weather report every day?"

Frustration filled his eyes as he shook his head and let out a heavy sigh.

"And one thing I know about you is that you only use shaving cream in a regular bathroom, not at a showering facility. You wouldn't have traveled with aftershave like that unless ..." Her jaw tensed as she fought back her looming tears, questioning whether he took SDC to New York after she declined, only to see her again today. "How could you?"

The stark break of silence built a chasm between them.

"Joy, listen to me!" he urgently cried out, but his words were lost in the wind. Chase helplessly stood there, mouth hanging open, as she hopped into her car and sped out of the parking lot.

In a state of shock and utter confusion, Chase watched helplessly as Joy vanished in a sea of cars. He immediately jumped in his truck and quickly maneuvered it toward the front of the parking lot. He anxiously patted his thumb against the steering wheel as he sat at the exit, observing oncoming traffic, waiting for a break long enough to safely enter the highway to catch up with his girlfriend.

Suddenly, he spotted his father across the street leaving Wynter's photography studio. Chase watched as Wynter and Phil walked towards his Bentley and affectionately embraced one another. After his father exited in the direction of the ranch, Chase clenched his teeth and made a sharp turn towards Joy's townhouse.

Chapter Eighteen

"ARE YOU GOING TO answer the door?" Tiana asked Joy as Chase rang the doorbell for the third time in a row. "What in the world happened between you two?"

"I'll tell you about it later." Restlessly, Joy paced back and forth before sneaking another glimpse out of the window at Chase's pickup truck, hoping that he would leave.

Tiana's attention immediately shifted towards the door as a knock echoed through the room. "It doesn't sound like he's going away."

"Well, he can stand out there all day for all I care." Joy crossed her arms and grunted.

"Joy, I need to leave for work. I can't be late." Tiana quickly zipped up her coat and checked the time on her phone. "Sorry, but I'm gonna have to open the door."

Their eyes met, and in that moment, a silent understanding passed between them. Being that she couldn't slip out through the garage because of where Chase had parked his truck, Joy surrendered, nodding as her arms flopped to her sides.

"*Okay*?" Tiana raised her eyebrows, seeking to confirm her friend's unspoken words.

"Yeah, I understand." Joy plopped onto the sofa and folded her arms again." He's not going to leave unless I talk to him anyway."

Tiana looked away, retrieved a small stack of papers from the kitchen table, and walked towards the front door. She accidentally clipped the edge of the console table that caused her work papers to tumble to the floor. Joy got up from the couch and headed towards her to help, but Tiana had already gathered her belongings. As she opened the front door, she watched Joy, who was still visibly upset, return to the sofa with a heavy sigh.

To Joy's surprise, Chase did not enter when Tiana left. Curious, she walked to the window overlooking the driveway and found them standing between each other's vehicles. Joy squinted as she tried to decipher their exchange that appeared as if they were trying to explain something to one another. *I hope he's not getting her involved...*

Joy released the bunched curtains gathered in her hand and walked to the front door. As she reached for the knob, she glanced down and saw the corner of a piece of paper. Joy picked it up and saw that it was stationery from where Tiana worked. She rushed out of the front door, guessing that it was something she needed. Just as she reached the end of the walkup, Joy saw Tiana back out of the driveway. She tried to wave her down, but Chase's truck blocked the view of the road. He locked eyes with Joy as she lowered her hand.

"Can we please talk?" he asked her with a genuine softness in his voice.

"I don't have anything to say to you." Joy rolled her eyes away from him as she completed an about face and marched back to her front door.

"Joy, I can explain," he said, following behind her. "Please, just let me explain."

When she reached her door, Joy stared at him before reluctantly allowing him inside. After she placed the paper on the table and retrieved her cell phone, she said to him, "I've got to call Tiana." After she dialed Tiana's number, Joy looked closer at the header on the paper, piecing together what she hadn't noticed before: Simpson Dialysis Center with the agency's initials, SDC, inside of a rectangular box.

Is she SDC? Joy searched her mind, recalling that the first few digits after the local area code of the number she found in her boyfriend's cupholder that night were indeed the same. Ignoring the hellos coming through the phone after the third ring, Joy abruptly ended the call and turned to face Chase.

With trembling lips and questions etched on her face, Joy tearfully asked, "Are you seeing Tiana?"

Chase closed his eyes, lowering his chin to the floor. He brushed his hand over his mouth and shook his head as he met her steady gaze. "No, I'm not. I would never do that to you."

"Let me see your phone." Joy stretched an open palm in his direction.

"Why?" Narrowing his eyes, Chase pulled off his baseball cap and tossed it onto the couch.

"If you have nothing to hide, let me see your phone," she insisted, now gesturing with her hand.

Without hesitation, Chase reached into his pocket and passed his phone to her. She quickly scrolled through his contacts and pushed the face of the screen in his direction. "Why do you have her work number saved in your phone as SDC?" Joy angrily glared at him. "Tell me the truth!"

"I'm telling you the truth!" he shouted back, angrily raising his voice at her for the first time in their relationship.

Joy flinched from his outburst. Gauging the tension in the air, Chase exhaled slowly, aiming to defuse it.

"I was planning something for you today," he said, his tone along with his facial expression, now noticeably softer. "Tiana was helping me to surprise you today."

"Surprise me?" Joy's eyebrows knitted together in confusion as she silenced Tiana's incoming return call on her cell.

"Yes, surprise you." Chase, hopeful that he had gotten through to her, pulled Joy towards him and wrapped his arms around her. "How could you think something like that?" He searched her eyes for understanding as he dried her tears with the back of his fingers. "I love you, Joy, and I would never lie to you. Don't you know that by now?"

Joy looked away from him, sniffling in response, torn between his words and the undeniable evidence before her. She had grown tired of being lied to by people she trusted, only to be left feeling foolish and betrayed. As she stared at him, Joy struggled with the possibility that he was being deceptive too.

Disappointed by her silence, Chase delicately traced the length of Joy's arms and released their embrace. He slowly picked up his baseball cap and started for the door. Before he turned the knob, Chase looked back at her.

"Just so you know, I did take a ride this morning at Greenfield's farm, not Greenland's. You've gotten them mixed up before." Chase steadied his gaze at her. "They have a slightly rockier ground than the muddier one when it rains." He had already emphasized to her the significance of his horses being able to navigate both terrains. Since he was riding one of his other horses, and not Impartially True, it was simply his personal riding preference, not the opinion of the professional who trained his prize-winning filly. "And they do have a shower installation, equipped with a jockey area, long extended counters and everything. Fairly new and pretty nice." He wet his lips, a mischievous smirk playing on his face as he said, "I put the aftershave on because I was meeting you for lunch. I know how much you like it. I can take you by Greenfield's if you'd like to see it for yourself."

Joy's lips were slightly parted as she stared at him, feeling embarrassed by her accusations.

"I'm coordinating a lease option to buy a few stable stalls because it's a closer ranch in state," Chase continued. "With all that I was trying to organize for you today, this morning was the only time I could go this week with everything going on. Not to mention the news I wanted to share at lunch." With a soft expression, his eyes brightened. "I just signed a new deal for the pieces I showcased in New York last month."

"*Oh, Chase...*" With a sense of regret, apologies poured from her eyes.

Chase gazed at Joy as he slowly walked back towards her. He gently tilted her chin upward and passionately kissed her like he had never done before. Joy closed her eyes and rested in his warm embrace. "When I say I love you," he spoke softly, "I really mean that I love you. I want *only* you. If you want the same thing, and only if you trust me," he emphasized, locking eyes with her, "meet me at LaGrange in two hours, wearing that dress I bought you for Christmas."

As Chase tenderly kissed her lips again, a rush of warmth spread through her body before he walked away, leaving her breathless.

———◇———

"Do you think she's going to show?" Patricia asked her brother as they stood off in a corner, side by side, near an elegantly arranged photo wall.

"I sure hope so." Chase tugged at the base of his handsewn cuffs, adjusting the slim fit dress shirt he wore. He looked towards the entrance of the restaurant, hoping to see Joy, only to find another relative arrive at his aunt's annual after New Year's celebratory bash. LaGrange's dining hall was temporarily closed to the public for their private dinner party this evening.

The intimate gathering of around fifty relatives, coordinated with meticulous care by Phil's sister, Virginia, was always a special and cherished occasion. The pass-the-mic party game engaged in each year was consistently the highlight of the evening, filled with laughter and unforgettable moments. Each family member participating in the game had to share something funny, heartfelt, or a lesson learned over the past year. Although the atmosphere was filled with warm displays of love and affection, it was equally enjoyable to hear the comedians in the family effortlessly inject bursts of hilarity into the occasion.

"What do you mean, *I sure hope so*?" Patricia glared at him.

"We had a *little* misunderstanding earlier, but I think it's all good with us now."

Patricia smacked him across the chest with the back of her hand. "What did you do?"

"Ow," he sharply wheezed, grimacing at his sister. "I didn't do anything." Chase massaged the center of his chest with the tips of his fingers. "And the next time you decide to hit me like that, please take those rings off first. They feel like brass knuckles."

Ignoring the pain she had inflicted, Patricia sternly pointed at him. "Joy is the one for you. What happened between getting your house all decorated for the private evening together and now?" She narrowed her eyes and hesitantly asked, "Was it Dad?"

Chase shook his head. "No, she hasn't even met him yet."

"Then it must've been the roommate thing, wasn't it?" she guessed.

Chase responded with a shrug, slowly easing out the word, "Maybe."

"I told you that was a bad idea." Patricia folded her arms. "What would you think if she had Booker's, or one of your close friend's numbers saved in her phone without you knowing about it? Especially under secretive initials."

"I get it, Pat, but you couldn't do it. Dad has had you buried in work since your maternity leave ended. After checking with a few of our cousins, Tiana was the only one available. Who else was going to help decorate?" Chase grunted. "I sure wasn't going to ask Mom. She's made it clear that her loyalty to Dad is solid as a rock, even after I told her what I saw earlier today. I still can't believe that she just hung the phone up on me." His eyes drifted across the exquisitely decorated room. "Where is she anyway?"

"Beats me." Patricia shrugged. "She was here a few minutes ago. Maybe she stepped out to use the restroom or something."

"Well, I want them all in this room when Joy gets here." Chase gently touched the pocket where the ring was securely tucked away for his girlfriend.

"Dad flipped a lid when Mom told him about the ring you bought." Patricia sighed and shook her head. "Are you sure you're doing the right thing by proposing here?"

"It's the only way. The problem Dad has with her skin color is his problem. Besides, how can I ask her to marry me and keep pretending that he doesn't exist? She deserves to know the truth."

"The truth?" Patricia's forehead wrinkled.

"Yeah, the truth about him, and the fact that I'm all in when it comes to her." Chase's expression softened. "I just can't see myself without Joy."

"I hear you, bro. It looks like she feels the same way too." Patricia smiled, her eyes lighting up as she looked towards the entrance where Joy had nervously appeared. "I think you better escort her in. She doesn't look very comfortable."

Chase stared, mesmerized by Joy's beauty, her aura arresting his attention. Approaching her, his gaze traveled from her flawless makeup to the elegant white dress that gracefully draped her figure. The flattering ruffles that cascaded on one side, accentuating her slim waistline, gently swayed with the subtle nervous pats to her thigh. The small, sparkling clutch purse she held was a perfect match with the heels she wore, adding a touch of glamour to her outfit. Her very presence brought a sense of sophistication to the room.

"Hey, babe, you look great," Chase whispered in Joy's ear, gently touching the nape of her neck that was exposed by her elegant updo.

"Hey," Joy softly responded, her voice barely above a whisper, with a bashful smile.

"I'm glad you came." He kissed her on the cheek and then guided her by the hand into the main dining area where his family was gathered.

"So, what's going on?" Joy glanced around at the mingling crowd of people, each in their own world.

"Well, this is what my aunt calls an after New Year's bash. I'll never understand why she has it on a Thursday evening, but that's just her. Aunt Virginia *really* enjoys the holidays." He chuckled. "Let's just say she hates to see it end." Chase pointed to the photos against the back wall. "She always highlights socials from December to remind us of how important family is. Sort of a family reunion."

Surveying the room once more, Joy quietly said, "But Chase, I'm not family." She was one of only three brown faces in a room filled with people. And the other two were a part of the waitstaff. "I don't know anyone here." She cast an inquisitive gaze upon him, feeling completely out of place.

Chase took her arm and intertwined it with his. "You know me, Patricia, and Mom. And you've met Paul and Booker. By the end of the night, everyone will know you." Chase winked at her, quietly observing his father enter the room.

Although Joy initially hesitated, her resistance faded as Chase took pleasure in introducing her to every person in the room, except Phil. Some of his family members even referred to Joy as a light in Chase's life, having heard so much about her before this meeting, and Booker had already taken a liking to her. Others raved about her sense of style and how well she complemented him. Joy enjoyed the funny stories some of them told regarding Chase's childhood and the embarrassing moments from his stint as a professional jockey. One cousin, Calvin, even pointed out the small scar, likened to a thin scratch, just at the edge of Chase's hairline from a fall he had as a teenager trying to show off.

With a sense of validation, Joy was flattered by how well received she was by his family, at least most of them. The hour they spent mingling amongst the other guests, nibbling on fluted edge hors d'oeuvres along the way, was an absolute delight. Everyone she met was cordial, even if some hadn't shown as much interest in meeting her as Calvin had.

"Are you having a good time?" Chase asked Joy, relishing her apparent happiness.

"Yes, I am." Joy nodded as she savored the last bite of the seafood dinner. "Your family is great. And this pass-the-mic thing is hilarious." She grinned, casting a smile across the table at Patricia who passed the mic to Chase.

"Well, it's not all laughs, some things are quite serious," he quietly said to her as he took the mic from his sister. Chase gazed into Joy's eyes as he spoke into the microphone, "Can I ask you a question?"

Joy momentarily glanced at Patricia, who wore a smile bigger than her brother's, and then back to Chase. Joy's heart raced and eyes widened as he got down on one knee. Suddenly, oohs and aahs came from the crowd. Some seated close enough were able to see what was happening, while others in the back relied on what was spoken into the microphone.

Chase set the mic on the table and reached into his pocket for the ring. When he pulled out the diamond and tilted it in Joy's direction, a hand snatched the mic from the table.

"This boy sure knows how to joke around," Phil said into the microphone. "My son, always the practical joker." He released a throaty laugh as he toggled the switch on the stem, turning the microphone off.

Chase could read the questions in Joy's eyes, a mixture of pain and confusion.

"Here, Booker, I think it's your turn." Phil gripped the microphone tighter as Chase discreetly tried to get it back from him, hoping to not cause too much of a scene. "What do you think you're doing?" Phil sharply whispered to Chase as he shoved the mic to his eldest son seated at the table behind them. "You're making a fool out of yourself," Phil harshly whispered with tightened lips.

"So, this is your father?" Joy asked Chase as she stared at Phil whose eyes showed contempt. She snatched her purse from the empty chair next to her and ran out of the room.

Chase's eyes narrowed as he pointed at Phil with indignation. "You are *not* going to stop me from marrying her!" He pushed Phil aside, shifting his eyes to Booker and then to his mother who had appeared behind them before he rushed out after Joy.

Lucille looked out over the crowd as she grabbed the microphone from Booker and turned it back on. "Hey, everybody," she said, her speech slurred, almost spilling the drink in her hand as she staggered. "I have something to share too."

Phil reached for the microphone in his wife's hand, but Lucille snatched away from him as she growled, "No, it's my turn!"

Everyone's attention was peeled on them as she staggered to the middle of the dance floor. "My dear husband of over thirty-three years has been keeping a little secret."

"Lucille, don't," he attempted to control her.

"Don't what, dear? We're all family here, right?" She woozily waved her hand in the air, motioning around the room. "Why don't you tell them about the new addition?"

"I'm sorry everyone, my wife has had way too much to drink," he apologized to his family. "Booker, help me get your mother home."

"No!" Lucille shuffled away, appearing to have a sobering moment. "You're not going to sweep this under the rug any longer. I've been having you followed. And I know all about your little tryst." She smugly raised her brows. "Uh-huh, I do … but there's one teensy weensy little thing I bet you didn't know." She dramatically measured an inch between her fingers for effect. "That's right, your little mistress is black! The same as the young lady you just ran out of here."

"I don't know what you're talking about." Phil tightened his full jaw as he glared at her.

"Oh, you don't?" Lucille mocked, and then pointed behind him. "Well, just check out the pictures I added to Virginia's photo wall." Phil abruptly turned towards the wall, as did his family, and analyzed the pictures she had clumsily thumbtacked to the satin wrapped corkboard. "My private investigator took *great* pictures of her and the little girl, too."

Phil's eyes widened as he struggled to accept the facts before him. There they were, prints of him and Wynter exiting his downtown office late at night, entering her photography studio with his hand on her lower back, and another of them embracing in the back parking lot of a hotel in a neighboring county during times when he had conveniently told his wife that he was out of town on business. However, it was only when he saw the picture of Wynter with a two-year-old who had remarkably similar features to him, his distinctive nose and cleft chin, that it dawned on him their connection, despite the child's slightly darker skin.

As Virginia enlisted the help of her children to defuse the commotion unfolding in the room, Lucille remained fixated on her husband's every move. "And yes, I know that she's upstairs right now," she whispered in his ear. "So ... don't come home tonight. I've sought counsel to challenge that prenup. After tonight, with the thirty plus years I've stood by your side, you don't stand a chance."

Lucille's hands trembled as she slammed her drinking glass to the floor, causing shards to scatter and heads to turn away from Virginia back towards her and Phil.

As his wife stumbled away, holding onto Booker and Patricia for support, Phil shifted his focus back to the pictures on display. He couldn't believe it as he slumped down to a nearby chair. It was a well-known fact between him and Wynter that she wasn't a natural blonde and her eyes weren't truly blue, but he had no idea that her fair skin would betray him in such a way.

He clutched his chest, reliving in his mind how she had cleverly convinced him to pay for her photography studio and new home in a recently developed subdivision. He partially blamed himself since he had practically begged her to move back to Alabama after her abrupt departure to Ohio years prior. It was only now that he realized that she had lied about losing their child together, and evidently, concealed her true identity of being biracial, born to a Caucasian mother and African American father, to pass as a white woman.

"Uncle Phil, are you alright?" Calvin asked, noticing the painful expression etched on Phil's face. No audible response came from him other than gasps of air. "Hey, somebody, call 9-1-1!"

Chapter Nineteen

JOY STARED OUT OF the window at the cascading waterfall pool. If she could ensure her immunity against the flu-inducing cold weather, she would happily take a swim to alleviate her worries. She stared down at the rock Chase had put on her finger, symbolizing their love for one another. On this memorable day, stemming from the vows they exchanged before God, destined to forever be etched in her memory, came an overwhelming sense of anticipation that caused butterflies to flutter in her stomach.

"Hey, Mrs. Carlington," Chase's voice boomed from behind her, the ink barely dry on their freshly signed marriage certificate.

Joy turned from the window and faced him as he emerged from the en suite bathroom wearing a thick beige towel securely tucked around his narrow waist. She had longed to hear those words ever since finding the ring in his dresser drawer she now wore.

"Hey, you," she whispered in his ear as he slid his arms around her waist.

"Wow, you're tense." With gentle circular motions, Chase massaged her back through the silky-smooth bathrobe.

"Yeah, I know. I'm a little nervous, for more reasons than one. I was so ready for this, but now my body is saying something different."

"I'll help you relax." His hands roamed from her back to the crest of her shoulder. Chase edged his fingers under the collar of her robe, easily revealing the lacey negligee he had bought the night before.

Joy flinched when he kissed her neck.

"Are you okay?" Chase questioned, noticing the reservations in her eyes.

Her gaze drifted from his to the vase of red roses on the nightstand and attractive basket of perfumed gifts stacked in a corner of the room. "I ... I just need a little bit of time." She gently rested her cheek against his chest.

Chase quietly exhaled in disappointment as he caressed her arms. "It's okay, we have all day ... I can wait."

Joy nodded as she intertwined her fingers with his and walked back toward the bench at the foot of the king-size bed.

"We can just talk for now, if you'd like. I know a lot has happened since last night." Chase sat beside her, recalling the phone call from his father just a few hours ago. "I hope that it's not the fact that my dad is in the hospital." He rested his hand on her knee. "None of this is our fault. And he's going to be okay." Chase sighed, having learned that Phil was already scheduled for release the next day.

Even from his sick bed, after emergency surgery to have a stent placement for his heart, Phil questioned him on a voice message about whether he had gone through with the engagement. Chase was resolved to prevent further interference from him in his relationship. Especially since he had managed to track Joy down in the parking lot of the hotel last night, where he finally proposed to her, creating a moment they would never forget. After a tearful night of intense conversations, the couple made the heartfelt decision to exchange vows at the courthouse this morning, despite the opinions of others.

"Aren't you worried about your father?" Joy questioned. "I mean, with surgery and everything, are you sorry that you turned your phone off last night?"

"No, besides, he's okay." With a sense of frustration, Chase released a heavy groan. "Don't get me wrong, I love my father, but I don't like him. And I'm not going to let him hurt you again. I promised your dad that I would protect you." He stared at her. "And that's a promise I plan to keep, no matter what."

With her brows knitted together, Joy scooted closer to him and questioned, "When did you talk to my dad?"

"It was back during Thanksgiving." Chase draped his arm across her shoulders. "Do you remember Black Friday when you went shopping with your mom and Elisha?"

"Yeah," she said, nodding. "I remember."

"Well, when I stayed behind with your dad, we talked. We actually talked for a long time." Chase reflectively grinned. "I told him about the ring I bought you and he shared with me how he saw it coming."

"Dad said that?" The corners of Joy's lips rose.

"Admittedly, he didn't think it would be so soon, but yes, he said that." Chase nodded, squeezing Joy's hand. "We couldn't hide it, even if we tried." Chase referenced their many displays of affection throughout that home visit. Occasionally absorbed in their own world, the two of them had to consciously remind themselves that they were not alone.

"And Dad was okay with us getting married?" Joy carefully swiped her hair behind her ears.

Chase groaned a bit before answering, "I didn't say that."

"Wait, what did he say then?" Her eyes showed concern.

"He was okay with my asking you. Mr. Maxwell made it clear that it was your decision to say yes ... or to say no."

Joy easily smiled, understanding her father's response. After she became an adult, Gerald often yielded to that school of thought. Although he would be there to guide her and her siblings, her father was adamant that he was not going to make decisions for them.

"And I'm glad you said yes." Chase rested his hand on her thigh. "Both last night when I asked, and this morning when we exchanged vows."

"Chase, I said I do to you in my heart long before the words were ever spoken." Joy scooted even closer to him and caressed the side of his face with subtle strokes of her thumb. "Thank you for being so patient with me." She slowly ran her fingers through the short fluffy strands of his freshly shampooed hair and kissed him. Softly, she whispered those three words, "I love you."

"I love you too," Chase gently replied, admiring how beautiful the ring looked on her finger. "So, why don't we listen to some music and just unwind. This day is about us." He gently patted her knee before he walked to the window and closed the blinds. Chase grabbed the remote from his dresser and turned on the surround sound speakers to their favorite mellow instrumentals. "After I get some clothes on, we can talk some more over my new drink I perfected for this occasion." Winking, he referenced the non-alcoholic strawberry sangria recipe he had mastered from the internet.

"Or we could just talk later," she softly said to him.

Joy rose from the bench and moved to the side of the bed, where she hadn't been since that night in November when she left for the guest bedroom, vowing to remain a virgin until her wedding day. The occasion was equally meaningful for Chase as he had maintained the same loyalty. Gracefully, she untied the sash of her robe and slipped out of the sleeves, allowing the garment to fall gently to the floor, revealing the short white negligee that clung to her curvaceous figure. She then carefully slid underneath the soft and inviting sheet, beckoning him with the slow motions of her forefinger.

Chase stared at her and instinctively dropped the remote in his hand, ignoring the batteries that popped out of the enclosure upon its impact on the floor. With long strides toward her from across the room, he eagerly approached their marital bed. Ever since he had developed a deep spiritual connection with Joy, Chase yearned to explore physical intimacy with the woman he had since envisioned as his wife. Today, with that vision realized, he slid underneath the sheet next to her.

With great anticipation, Chase gazed as Joy extinguished the lights on the nightstand, rendering her delicate state completely into his care.

Chapter Twenty

THE WARM SPRING AIR at Churchill Downs was optimal weather for the horse race of the year. With the top performers in the industry in attendance, there were murmurings of Impartially True's unfavorable odds. Despite this, Chase, along with his horse's devoted trainer, jockey, and groom, qualified for the hard-fought trip to Kentucky.

The women in the audience made the event even more memorable, turning heads with their extravagant displays of hats, creating a show within a show. With elegance, Joy wore her stylish white hat, which served as both a fashionable accessory and a practical shield from the sun. As the gates flung open at the start of the race, everyone's eyes were glued to the track.

"Come on, Impartially True!" Joy yelled as the horses blazed around the racetrack for the legendary competition. She was just as fired up about the filly Chase had invested so much in as he was. "Come on!" she shouted with a voice full of urgency, drowning in the thunderous chants of the crowd as his horse neared the front of the pack.

"Yeah, yeah, yeah!" Chase was on his feet, next to his wife, with clenched fists and a pounding heart as he rooted for his horse. In a jockey pose, his legs were crouched, mirroring the intense energy of the horse's final stretch, blazing to a hairline victory just at the two-minute mark.

"Yes!" Chase howled, thrusting his fist into the air. He hugged Joy, almost tipping the wide brim hat off her head.

"You did it!" While securely holding her hat in place to prevent it from falling, Joy bounced with excitement as Chase held onto her. "Oh my God, we won!"

Chase briefly placed his hand on Joy's stomach as he said, "Yes, *we* won," reflecting on the news Joy shared with him months prior.

Patricia gripped a handful of Paul's shirt sleeve, excitedly tugging him back and forth before hugging Joy and Chase with bouts of hysterical laughter in between.

Moments later, cameras and reporters crowded around Chase, pouring out congratulations as the owner of the underrated filly in the sport. Impartially True proved to be a healthy contender and ready for the victory at Churchill Downs today. Chase recognized the unwavering commitment of his jockey and trainer, who stood by him during the many challenges faced over the past six months, resulting in finding a secure home for his horses and a successful victory for Impartially True. Waving his hand, he signaled for Travis to join the group of honorees, acknowledging the integral part he had played in it all. It took a village to achieve the triumph they had today.

As Chase fielded interviews from various media outlets alongside Impartially True's trainer, Joy stood next to him in the winner's circle, reflecting on her own recent accomplishments. In addition to securing contracts for her growing business, Joy celebrated her graduation ceremony that took place just a week prior with her entire family in attendance. They had since gotten over the initial shock that she was now a married woman, but when Phil unexpectedly approached her at the conclusion of the service, everyone was stunned at his presence.

"Are you ready to go?" Chase asked, shattering Joy's thoughts as he motioned Patricia and Paul, who were several yards away, toward the exit. "I'm sure you and the little one are ready for a bite to eat." He pecked her on the cheek as he interlocked his fingers with hers.

Joy gently smiled at him and nodded. "Yes, we are." She chuckled, walking quickly to keep pace with him. "Ever since my morning sickness passed, I feel like I can eat a horse."

"Hey," he nudged her with his elbow, "don't let anyone hear you say that around here."

Glancing at the horses being led back to the stables, Joy cringed. "Sorry, I forgot where I was."

"I see that." Chase grinned as they left the racetrack.

On the ride back to the hotel after a celebratory dinner party, Joy pondered what Phil had said at her graduation. When Chase saw his father approaching them from the rear of the building, he stood in front of Joy while her family promptly stopped his steady advance. Despite Phil's prior apologies to Chase, they were all prepared for the worst when he reached into the front of his jacket.

"You've barely said two sentences since we've been in the car." Chase shook Joy's knee. "What are you over there thinking about?"

She exhaled a deep breath and looked in his direction. "Last week. I'm still trying to process what happened."

Chase nodded, mirroring his own surprise at his father's actions. After months of dodging Phil's calls, he had finally agreed to meet with him a couple days before Joy's graduation. One reason was that he learned his father had been readmitted to the hospital due to complications arising from underlying health conditions, but Phil was again promptly released the next afternoon. Another reason was that he felt his father had undergone a personal change. After his mother revealed that she had forgiven him once again and taken him back after things abruptly ended between him and Wynter, this time she shared that he had left the exclusive club he had been a part of for the past twenty plus years.

"I know. Up until your graduation, I was still trying to figure out if it was real." Chase grunted to himself. "But when Booker called and told me that morning that he was helping him clean out his office, he said that the flag was gone."

"What flag?" Joy gazed at him with curiosity.

Chase struggled to convey the depth of loyalty his father displayed towards the Confederate flag and the dark side of the era it represented. For Phil, it went beyond a historical symbol of the past, but rather a celebrated display for segregation—until he met his daughter, Autumn, for the first time. The ice in his heart began to melt each time he was forced to face the fact that his blood was running through this innocent child. No number of paternity tests, and he had taken three, could delegitimize her direct relation to him. None.

After he came to terms with that fact and the change occurring in his heart, Phil settled the details of child support with Wynter out of court, compromising on summer and holiday visits. They came to an agreement where, in exchange for liquidation of the properties she had acquired from him and, at Lucille's urging, Wynter's agreement to move back to Ohio, Phil would provide a new home there and pay a set monthly sum until their daughter reached the age of maturity.

"The Confederate flag," Chase cautiously disclosed to his wife. "The Confederate flag that hung on a wall in his home office was gone."

"Oh..." Joy's demeanor changed as her gazed drifted out of the window.

"Yeah, so, I don't know. A flag removed from the wall doesn't mean that he's truly changed, so I'm treading lightly with this one."

"Do you think what he gave me was all for show?" Joy questioned, looking back at Chase.

"Only God can answer that, Joy. I've known my father all my life and I'm still trying to figure him out. Mom believes him,

Booker and Patricia too," he sighed, "but I'm not fully there yet."

"But do you forgive him?" she carefully asked.

Chase swallowed hard as they stopped at a traffic light. "I have to, right? Being a Christian, isn't that what I'm supposed to do?" With a penetrating gaze, his eyes sought agreement.

Joy released a labored sigh. "But you should also want to," she reminded him. "Forgiveness is for you, not him."

"I know," Chase nodded, "and I do forgive him. I did from the moment I visited him in the hospital the first time he was admitted. I just can't say that I trust him. You know what I mean?" He methodically tapped his thumb on the steering wheel, checking his blind spot before switching lanes to make a right turn into the hotel parking lot where they were staying for the night. "What about you?"

"Yes, I have," Joy answered. "And it doesn't have anything to do with him giving me Wynter's studio," she admitted. "I can't be bought. It's because I saw something different in him than I did that night you proposed. There is no way a man who has lived a life like you've described and said some of the horrible things about me, and my people, could publicly admit how wrong he's been. I mean, Chase, he was in tears last week. If he hadn't changed, why would he come to my graduation, knowing that my family would be there too?"

Chase didn't have an explanation for that. When Phil reached into his jacket, it took everything in Zachary to not tackle him on the spot. Gerald placed a hand on his son's arm, edging his other son, Joshua, back as well, as Phil raised his hands in defense. As his eyes drifted between the group of people in Joy's corner, Phil realized his mistake. When he finally handed her the folded deed for the property, along with an apology, the tension between them eased.

"Maybe to pacify his guilty conscience." Chase grunted as he parked his rental in a space near the front entrance of the hotel. "Mom told me about the nightmares he's been having. After that heart attack when she took him back in, she told me that there have been nights when he's woken up screaming, sweating like he's been out in the rain. There have been times when she found him crying in the shower, and he even asked her to pray with him. That's just not like him."

"But isn't that what change is?"

Chase met his wife's gaze, his shoulders lowering as he sighed. "Yeah, I guess so. But what about your family?"

"Listen, my parents are okay with him coming to the reception they've planned for us. I won't pretend that everything is perfect, but it'll look pretty bad to have several of your family members there and not him. Especially after he's expressed how sorry he is." Joy recounted what it took for her family to come to terms with their private wedding at the courthouse. And now, she just wanted to avoid any drama that could overshadow their formal wedding reception and the excitement of being pregnant with their first child.

"I understand what you're saying. It's just that when I think about all I've already forgiven him for, I wonder if he'll just backslide and do it again."

"How many times did Jesus say we are to forgive?"

Chase released a soft chuckle. "Seventy times seven."

"Okay, then." Joy gently smiled at him as she unbuckled her seatbelt. "Unless you plan on counting the number of times you've forgiven him before, try to see him for who he is today."

THE LUXURIOUS GOLD-FOIL ENGRAVED invitations served as an elegant centerpiece, nestled in a bed of tangerine and white roses, for each guest table at the sunset event. Margaret was thrilled that the backyard renovations were completed just in time to transform it for her youngest daughter's wedding reception. As loved ones gathered for the occasion, the beautifully decorated air-conditioned tent, strung with twinkling lights, came alive with the sounds of laughter and upbeat music from the live band.

Instead of the traditional rehearsal dinner usually held the night before a wedding, Joy was treated to an elaborate combination bridal baby shower that left her speechless. Anything but ordinary, the lavish affair held at the five-star hotel in Lewiston Springs filled with surprises and extravagant gifts, topped her expectations. With Michelle and Tiana working in tandem with

Elisha and Charity, it soon became one of the most cherished moments for Joy that she will always hold dear.

Gerald rested his arms around Margaret's shoulders and smiled. The view he shared with his wife was one he had prayed for since they started a family. All five of their children mingled in the crowd, some dancing while others engaged in lively conversations. He wanted to see them all happy and in loving relationships with spouses that would treat them as God intended.

With Elisha and Tyler, he recalled how young he and Margaret were when they met. They too met in grade school and love blossomed from the innocence of their youth. With Charity and Milton, Gerald pondered the bond that was unbreakable between him and Margaret... no matter what. They too had broken up at one time prior to marriage, a little-known fact to their children, albeit very brief.

During that time, he realized that there was no other woman for him. Even though they occasionally disagreed, they both recognized that disagreements for them never led to fights. As he matured, Gerald understood that disagreements were something all couples encountered at one time or another. It was inevitable. Their occasional differences didn't indicate a lack of compatibility. Rather, they simply served as reminders that they were two unique individuals coming together as one.

His sons, Joshua and Zachary, epitomized the strength and integrity he had hoped they would embrace. Their growth from boys to young men prompted him to think about the Scripture in 1 Corinthians 13:11: *When I was a child, I spoke as a child, I understood as a child, I thought as a child; but when I became a man, I put away childish things.* They had each matured in their own ways and became staunch providers and fierce protectors of their households.

And his baby girl, Joy, aptly named for the spirit she possessed, Gerald couldn't help but smile every time he looked at her. As he remembered her senior year in high school, the year he stopped traveling abroad to spend more time with her before she left for college, Gerald caressed his wife's shoulders. Margaret kissed him on the cheek and gently rested her head against his. He fondly cherished the dinner dates and intimate father-daughter conversations they shared over her favorite dessert, strawberry smothered cheesecake with a dollop of whipped cream.

The picture of her enjoying this dessert for the first time as a three-year-old was still in a special frame on a display shelf in their living room. But even without the physical reminder, that image would forever be etched in his mind. He chuckled to himself as he thought about the whipped cream perched on the tip of her nose. When Margaret added a small piece of cherry nestled into the cream, he made it a point to capture the moment. Now, Joy was a professional photographer, capturing moments like that for others.

No longer his little girl, Joy was now Chase's wife. A marriage that began without the presence of family members, but certainly with the One who ordained it. As unconventional as it was for him, Gerald was proud of both her and Chase for making a decision that was solely theirs to make. Although he longed to walk her down the aisle, reminiscing about the time he had done so for his other daughters, Gerald smiled at what Joy told him. When she had shared the message from God in her heart, it became evident that her dream wedding did occur as it was beyond earthly imagination. Although they didn't have parents, siblings, aunts, uncles, and the like, being saved and committed to God, they did have a heavenly cloud of witnesses.

"Gerald, they're calling for you." Margaret jostled his knee and shook him from his thoughts. "It's time for the father-daughter dance."

"Oh, my mind was somewhere else." He chuckled heartily and carefully smoothed the front of his suit against his body as he approached Joy who extended her hand to him.

She gracefully stood in the middle of the dance floor, flaunting her sparkly off-the-shoulder evening gown that concealed her small, growing bump, sure that the hired photographer would capture the best angle of her pose.

Gerald waved as the guests clapped their hands as if he were on stage again during his Gospel touring days and took his daughter's hand. They happily danced as the band played a lively, upbeat song. When he looked at her, for a fleeting moment, he saw his twelve-year-old with braces and a radiant smile. He fought to suppress the tears welling in his eyes.

When the song changed and Chase approached them in the center of the dance floor, Gerald patted him on the back and placed Joy's hand in his. He kissed his daughter on the cheek and slowly walked away. Others gathered on the dance floor as Margaret joined her husband near the newlyweds.

"You're feeling what I felt earlier, aren't you?" she whispered in his ear, recalling her teary-eyed moment just before the guests arrived.

"I guess I am." Gerald grinned with embarrassment. "I just didn't think I'd feel this way."

"Well, we didn't have much time to process the whole thing." Margaret followed Gerald's lead as they swayed to the music. "One day we're planning a graduation dinner, and the next we find out that she's married and pregnant."

"It was a surprise, but at least it was in that order."

"Yeah, but I still wanted my baby to stay a baby for just a little while longer." Margaret playfully pouted as she fidgeted with his lapel before laying her hand flat against his chest.

"Soon enough, she'll be bringing one home to us."

"I know…" Margaret watched as Joy rested her head on Chase's chest. He carefully cradled her in his arms with closed eyes and relaxed his cheek over the crown of her head. "And he will be surrounded by love."

Gerald glanced at Phil who was swaying to the beat with Lucille in his arms. "Yes, he will," he said with a smile, eagerly anticipating the arrival of their grandson later in the fall.

Gerald's fixed gaze on Lucille and Phil was noticed by Chase. He watched as his parents danced together in a warm embrace. It was a loving sight to behold. Before Phil truly dedicated his life to Christ and stopped pretending to be saved by simply showing up at church, he admitted that he saw his soul going to hell. The haunting nightmares that kept him awake at night and his two life-threatening experiences served as stark wakeup calls. The deep-seated hatred in his heart could only be rooted out by the Savior, Jesus Christ. And with Phil's total submission to Him, it was.

Chase remembered how Phil encouraged him after Impartially True failed to place in the two following Triple Crown races, urging him to move his horses back home. Although hesitant at first, Chase finally agreed after getting the details of their agreement in writing. Nearly two months since the Kentucky Derby win, with Phil noticeably forty pounds lighter, the father and son now regularly meet for weekly horse rides together to further mend their relationship.

As the celebration neared an end, the family gathered for multiple group pictures. The last photograph, though, captured the essence of the Maxwell family. With Joy and Chase centered, surrounded by those who had grown and was growing to love one another, they all smiled, embracing where they were in life: a group of imperfect people, loving the one perfect God.

Infallible

Love never fails...
1 Corinthians 13:8a

———◆○◆———

About the Author

RENÉE ALLEN MCCOY, a loving wife and mother of two children, has a passion to share the Gospel of Jesus Christ. In addition to having work featured in national publications, she has penned several titles.

With a heart to tell stories that will not only entertain, Renée hopes to enlighten readers to capture the message and power of God's saving grace.

Feel free to visit her online at www.ReneeAllenMcCoy.com to join her email list and for more information on upcoming releases.